GIDEON'S RIVER

"Gideon's river" is London's river, the Thames, main artery of life and trade for twenty million people—main artery, too, for much crime and many criminals. In charge of all the police forces who guard the river is George Gideon, Commander of London's Criminal Investigation Department. Concentrated into a comparatively short period in high summer, this narrative tells of crimes planned and carried out; of crimes thwarted; of personal tragedies and triumphs. Of the many powerful, compelling themes, the most dramatic is that of the fashion show, prepared in great secrecy. A vast fortune in jewels and furs is to be displayed in a great river parade . . . while thieves wait and watch for their moment to strike, and the police get little warning . . .

Books by J. J. Marric in the Ulverscroft Large Print Series:

GIDEON'S RISK · GIDEON'S LOT
GIDEON'S POWER · GIDEON'S WEEK
GIDEON'S DAY · GIDEON'S RIVER

This Large Print Edition
is published by kind permission of
HODDER AND STOUGHTON LTD.
London

Gideon's River

J. J. MARRIC

Complete and Unabridged

ULVERSCROFT
Leicester

First printed in Great Britain 1968

First Large Print Edition
published April 1973
SBN 85456 179 X

This special large print edition is
made and printed in England for
F. A. Thorpe, Glenfield, Leicestershire

The characters in this book are entirely imaginary and bear no relation to any living person

CONTENTS

Chapter One

BIG SHIPS, LITTLE SHIPS

They came into the Port of London from every corner of the world, the big ships and the little ships, the tankers and the tugs, the liners and the banana boats, the modern ships and the old. They came by day and by night, hindered only by the tides, or by fog; or on those days when the men who worked the docks withdrew their labour in protest for some cause, probably real and vital to them, but often mysterious and frustrating to the rest of London.

For London and all Londoners depended on the Port of London for more than they realised; in fact the Thames was the lifeblood of the nation's capital. Muddy and grey near the open sea and at its wide, waiting estuary, in the upper reaches it was clear as a mountain stream. Far up, even as far as Hammersmith and Putney, Richmond and Teddington, the laden barges sailed their sluggish way with coal and wood and grain and oil and countless other vital goods which could be taken by water more cheaply than by rail or road. At Tilbury where the great stretch of docks began, no bridge spanned the river; but the Pool of London was made by the Tower and by London Bridge as well as by London's history.

But not only was the river the highway for the food which fed the nation, it could also be the highway for those who fed on crime. True, there was much more crime on the land on either side than on the river itself, but much of that crime started on the river, and it was sometimes difficult to understand where responsibility began and ended for the investigation into crimes committed on land or on water, on docks or in warehouses, in pubs or in pleasure boats.

In fact, four police forces controlled the river, all working closely together.

On the broad expanse of the water itself the Thames Division of the Metropolitan Police was in control, its ceaseless patrol of small boats and swift launches keeping a constant vigil both day and night. One small stretch of water, from Tower Bridge to the Temple, was however controlled partly by the City of London Police; but the two forces acted as one in the defence of London's property and people.

The docks which led off the river, docks with such names as Royal Albert and Victoria, London and Saint Katharine, Surrey and Millwall, were walled and protected like mediaeval cities, with policemen at the gates to check and control the lawful flow of lorries and carts, dockers and lightermen, port authority and Customs officers. These docks were protected by a different force, the police of the Port of London Authority, who had a close and intricate knowledge of the wharves and warehouses, quays and berths, repair shops, storage sheds and transport.

These police worked in the closest co-operation with the other two forces having the same objectives, rules and grievances, the same sense of dedication too seldom understood by civilians who worked in or on the river, and beyond.

Finally, there were the Customs men, two groups, each dealing with quite different aspects of the business of London: the Landing Branch who dealt with cargo only, and the Water Guard who dealt with ships' stores, passengers and crew.

If in fact the Customs force could be regarded as two forces, then the Metropolitan Police should be also, for the Thames Division with their reefer jackets, white shirts and white collars and their caps, were quite distinct in appearance if not in purpose; so, in all, six different forces of police guarded different parts of London's river.

Occasionally, very occasionally, each of these became involved in the same crime and the same series of crimes.

Probably none of the others would ever have admitted it, happy though their relations were with one another, but when all six became involved the man in overall command was likely to be the Commander of the Criminal Investigation Department of the Metropolitan Police—George Gideon. He would have been the last to claim control and yet, subconsciously, would no doubt have exerted it. And the other branches, knowing and accepting the need for co-ordination as well as co-operation, would almost certainly have accepted his authority without question.

On the night when a certain series of crimes began on the river, Gideon was at home, with his wife and one of their six children. He was "on call"—he was nearly always on call. He was always instinctively aware that, in the London he so loved, during every minute of the day and night some crime was being planned or committed; and that any one of these crimes might bring a time of great testing for any one of London's police forces. He was not consciously pre-occupied with that at this particular moment, however. An exceptionally pretty girl with an exceptionally nice figure was singing an exceptionally ugly tune on television. Kate, Gideon's wife, noticed the intentness with which Gideon watched, and smiled affectionately to herself.

Mary Rose was also an exceptionally pretty girl with an exceptionally nice figure. She should have been light-hearted and gay, as the singer appeared to be. Instead, she was terrified. She had been terrified ever since Tom and Dave had started to quarrel in the pub. Tom had sneaked her away, hoping that Dave wouldn't notice; but he had. They had cut across a building site, hearing the engine of Dave's car start up, knowing he was giving chase. Tom had dashed down the alley leading to the quay steps, but Dave might have seen them from the car, there was no way of being sure.

She stood at the bottom of the steps, hearing the river water slapping the stone walls and plopping against the sides of a small boat. Tom was standing in the boat, unsteadily, half-drunk. Across the water a few lights showed at warehouses and barges, some distance up-river a pub was gay with coloured lamps. Now and again a car or lorry passed along the road behind them, lights ghostly in the gloom, but none stopped. Perhaps one was Dave's; perhaps they were safe.

Mary Rose could just make out Tom's lean figure as he sat down. She heard sounds she could identify, of oars grating on the rowlocks. Another car came along the road, its engine very clear. She turned her head and stared up towards the top of the steps.

"Come on!" Tom whispered.

"I—I daren't!"

"Come on, don't waste time!"

"I—I can't, I'm too scared!" she gasped.

"You'll be more scared if they catch you," he growled hoarsely. "They're so drunk they'll do anything. We've got to get away."

"Tom, I—"

"Are you coming or aren't you?" he demanded, his roughness cloaking his own fear. "If Dave catches you while he's drunk, he'll slash your face to pieces."

"Oh, God," she gasped. "Don't say it!"

"Come *on*, then, get a move on."

He was right, she knew. Dave would slash her, she would lose her beauty she would be scarred for life. He had slashed other girls. Taking a timid step forward on to the green slime on the step, she nearly fell.

The car slowed down.

"It's them!" cried Tom, in anguish. "Are you coming, or aren't you?"

A car door slammed, and another. Footsteps sounded, sharp and urgent. Mary Rose leaned against the wall and groped with her right foot for the boat. Now Tom was leaning forward, hand outstretched to help her. She took it.

"*Jump!*" he urged.

She could not make herself jump, but she clambered over, crouching, scraping her legs and knee painfully, ruining her stockings. Footsteps clattered in the narrow cut leading to the steps, hard leather and metal hell-tips on the uneven cobbles. Tom sat back and pushed with one oar against the wall. The boat rocked, and Mary Rose gave a little groan. Tom slid the oar back into the rowlock and started to row. The clatter drew nearer, and drowned another sound on the river itself—the even beat of the engine of a motor-boat, some distance away.

The rowing boat was only ten yards from the steps when a torch shone out, bright beam dazzling. When Mary Rose twisted round she saw behind it only darkness, but the beam shifted and shone on the oily-looking surface of the river. Another torch beam cut the darkness like a knife.

A man called: "There they are!"

"See them?"

"There's Mary Rose!"

The light shone on the back of her head then passed either side. losing itself in the mirror of water. Something fell heavily close to the boat; plonk. Tom rowed desperately, but did not seem to draw any nearer to safety. Mary Rose, feeling the boat rocking more and more, held tightly to the sides. One torch went out but the other focussed on her, and something thudded into the side of the boat.

"They're throwing beer bottles," Tom muttered.

Beer bottles . . .

They must have brought beer bottles to smash and jab into her face and Tom's face. All this, for a kiss and a hug—not knowing Dave had been in the pub. Oh, God!

"Why don't you get out into the river?" she gasped. "We're too close."

"I'm—I'm rowing as hard as I can."

"We're closer than we were!" she muttered in sheer terror; and as if he had heard her a man on the bank said clearly:

"They'll never make it, Dave."

"Never thought they would," another man said. He raised his voice. "Come and get it, you whore! Come and get it."

"Tom—Tom, row *harder*!"

"They're in an eddy—" it was the first man speaking—"going round in circles, see?" Both men began to roar with laughter.

It was true, they *were* going round in circles, Mary Rose realised in awful fear. That was why they were no further from the steps.

The man with Dave spoke clearly. "I got an idea, Dave."

"What's that?"

"Sink 'em," the man said, simply.

"Sink 'em?" echoed Dave.

No, oh no, no!

"There's these old barrels, right here," the man with Dave remarked. "Roll 'em down the steps, that would rock the boat all right."

"Not a bad idea," Dave said, with drunken intentness. "I'd rather carve them up, but they'll be better off dead."

Oh, God, why had this happened to her?

"Come on!" the second man said. "Let's get them rolling."

The torch light changed direction, pitched on to the steps and showed the dark silhouettes of the men. Dave's long hair was like a wig—a golliwog's hair. Tom rowed more desperately than ever but was gasping for breath and could not get the boat away; he never would, now. Mary Rose sat in numbed despair, not even praying. She heard the men on the steps moving about, and suddenly something came crashing down on them and hurtled into the water. There was a great splash, and the boat keeled over very steeply.

Mary Rose screamed.

Again Dave's friend roared with laughter. "One more will do it!" he bellowed. "Heave, there, heave!"

Then without warning, a bright light shone out from the river and a glow of light appeared in the road behind the steps. An engine roared, making a strange echo on the river, and a patrol boat drew close to the steps and the helpless couple. Another clatter of footsteps sounded on the steps.

"It's the cops," Tom gasped. "It's the bloody cops."

Observing lights and unaccustomed activity at Fiddler's Steps, the Thames Division patrol report read, we called assistance from the land and a car moved on to the source of the trouble from land while we approached by water. Two arrests were made. David Carter and Samuel Cottingham were subsequently charged with attempting to cause grievous bodily harm to Mary Rose Shamley and Thomas Argyle-Morris by attempting to sink the boat they were in and throwing bottles at them. The charges were made at . . . It was a short report, giving no idea of the skill required by the patrol to approach the steps so cautiously, nor of the almost instinctive way in which the patrol had first noticed that something unusual was happening, and had called for help from land. Scissors operations like this between Thames Division, N.E. Division and the City of London were so common that no one thought it worth special comment.

When the first morning daylight patrol of the river between Greenwich and Blackfriars Bridge was about to start off, "Old Man River" Singleton, who was in charge at Divisional H.Q., strolled down the ridged gangway towards the landing stage where three vessels were moored. The three-man crew was already aboard. One was a bearded sergeant, at the helm, the second an elderly constable, and the third a youngster who had been in the Thames Division for little more than a year.

"Take a close look at Fiddler's Steps, Tidy, and examine that dinghy. If there are scratches where the bottles struck, we need to know."

"Right sir."

"When will that pair be charged?" the young man asked.

"Teach him his ABC," Singleton said, caustically.

There was a general laugh; any policeman who forgot that the charge would follow in the morning as day followed night, really did need to go back to school.

The patrol boat moved off, slowly, into mid-stream and then up-river.

Behind it was the magnificence of Tower Bridge and the Pool beyond, seen through the grey stone frame of the two main pillars of the arch. The sun, rising above the roof tops of warehouses and the spidery tops of cranes, brightened the masts and the bridge of a Uruguayan ship of about seven thousand tons which was unloading grain.

"Ships are beginning to use the river a bit more than they did, not going into the docks so much," remarked Sergeant Tidy. "There was a Frenchie at Hay's yesterday and a Yank at London."

He spoke casually as he scanned the ruffled surface of the river. Fiddler's Steps were only a few hundred yards down, not far below Wapping Old Stairs, and "taking a close look" would be the first job; they could almost drift towards the spot on this ebb tide. A piece of driftwood clunked against the propeller, but none of the men took any notice when the boat shuddered. Some straw and a cigarette carton drifted past, the carton making a splash of crimson against the yellow straw. They saw this as they saw everything—the still and silent barges moored in the roads, the men working on wharves and in warehouses, here and there a car close to the water's edge. Everything on the river and on the banks appeared to be normal, the sun was beginning to catch the water, giving it a beauty they did not fully understand. A tanker from Holland, of three or four thousand tons, passed them up-river; none of the crew gave it more than a cursory glance.

The patrol boat drew closer to Fiddler's

Steps, where a floating barrel was bumping gently against the wall of the recess by the side of the steps; another, further away, was trapped in a kind of pontoon of driftwood which had collected in a corner, as a result of an eddy which was always here at high tide. The little row-boat, one of the few still used to reach barges which had become loose in the roads, was moored to a ring in the wall of the steps.

The youngest man, Addis, said: "What's that?"

"What's what?" asked Sergeant Tidy.

"That." Addis pointed towards the pontoon, and following his gaze, his companions saw a small brown packet caught in the driftwood. Tidy turned the boat, but they could not get near enough to pick it out by hand. Addis unhooked the hitching pole and prodded for the packet, caught it and drew it in cautiously. The elderly constable leaned over and picked it out of the water.

"That's a special waterproof container—look how it's sealed," Addis remarked. The constable turned it over, and saw a faint ring on one side but made no comment.

"Wonder what's in it?" said Addis.

"Tell you what," said Tidy, "we'll take that straight back and let Old Man River open it and find out." He throttled hard, turned the boat swiftly, and raced back towards the landing stage.

Chapter Two

SCOTLAND YARD

At Scotland Yard that morning, there was a curious sense of alertness, almost of tension, which developed without warning and lasted for a few minutes two or three times each day. It was never quite possible to explain it. Certainly George Gideon, Commander of the Criminal Investigation Department, did not want to create such an atmosphere when he arrived to start the day's work, but inevitably he did so. The only other man who had this effect was the Commissioner, Colonel Sir Reginald Scott-Marle, and this sometimes puzzled Gideon for he did not see himself in any way like the aloof, austere soldier who directed the affairs of the Metropolitan Police with military detachment from its men. In fact, most of the Force held Scott-Marle in awe, although some would never have admitted it. Without exception, they held Gideon in deep respect. Whether he liked it or not, and sometimes he disliked it very much indeed, he had become a kind of father figure at the Yard.

On that particular morning, a stranger might have understood why he earned such respect and gave the impression of almost paternal benevolence. Stepping out of his car, big, heavily-built, with thick shoulders and a big head thrust slightly forward, iron grey hair brushed back from his forehead like thick, crinkly wire, he gave an impression of power. As a man hurried forward to hold the door for him, however, the stern expression on his face altered, he smiled and said casually:

"Hello, Simms. How's that daughter of yours?"

Simms, as old as Gideon and still a sergeant, was craggy-faced and burly. His eyes lit up.

"Fine, sir, thank you."

"Did she have those twins?"

"False alarm, sir, but a whopping big boy. Nearly ten pounds he was."

"Don't know how they do it these days." Gideon said, nodded, and started up the high flight of stone steps towards the main hall. A uniformed man saluted.

"Good morning, sir."

’Morning, ’morning, good morning, ’morning.

Footsteps rang out on the cement floor, voices all held a hollow ring in the bare passages.

’Morning. Good morning sir. ’Morning, ’Morning, ’Morning.

Gideon opened the door on the right, and a shaft of sunlight struck him in the face. He put his hand up to shade his eyes quickly, blinking, and went to his desk. It was empty and almost forbidding, the IN, OUT, PENDING, in fact all the trays shiny and polished. He was not yet used to Hobbs as his second-in-command, instead of Lemaitre, who had served him for so many years. Hobbs, with his sturdy old English name, was the public school and university man; Lemaitre, with a name which had come over with the Huguenots, was a cockney to his marrow. Gideon, who had recommended Hobbs for the post of Deputy Commander and was still sure he had been right, nevertheless felt a certain nostalgia. Until a few weeks ago the desk in the corner would have been littered, Lemaitre would have been sitting there with his colourful bow tie, his slightly beady but alert eyes, his lined and wrinkled face. And a pile of reports would have been on Gideon's desk with some notes on top, all in Lemaitre's copperplate hand.

Now it was almost too tidy.

The door opened, slowly.

"Good morning," Hobbs said.

He carried a batch of reports under his arm, in a much tidier parcel than Lemaitre's had ever been. He was a compact, dark-haired man with regular features, dark grey eyes, and a touch of severity about an expression culled more from Scott-Marle's background than Gideon's. But he was a dedicated policeman. Some older men at the Yard disliked him but none denied that he had met them on their own ground, in the detection of crime, and beaten them. A year as Superintendent of one of the East End's toughest divisions had proved his quality beyond all doubt.

Ever since they had met, there had been moments when Gideon felt slightly ill-at-ease with Hobbs, and those moments had become rather more frequent during the period since Hobbs' wife had died. In a strange way it was as if part of Hobbs had died with her, and Gideon was seldom wholly free from a sense of awkwardness; but it never showed.

"'Morning, Alec," he said. "What have we got this morning?"

"Nothing of special interest," Hobbs said. "Only two new cases we need worry about." He implied that the rest of London's crime could be dealt with that morning by the men out in the divisions. "Van Hoorn is coming over from Amsterdam about the industrial diamond smuggling; he seems certain that the diamonds are coming into England."

"Does he say why he's certain?"

"Only that they've caught one of the thieves, a man known to fly to and from London regularly." Hobbs put a file on Gideon's desk, fairly full and fat. Gideon opened it and saw a typewritten note summarising what Hobbs had just said, and finishing: *Inspector Van Hoorn is due at London Airport on Flight 1701 KLM Airlines at eleven-fifteen this morning.*

"Who are you sending out to meet him?" asked Gideon.

"I thought you might like to go."

"No, thanks!"

"Then Micklewright."

Gideon conjured up a mental image of a tall, spare, sandy-haired Detective Superintendent who was one of the Yard's experts on precious stones and whose knowledge of diamonds was a by-word.

"He's not very good with foreigners," he remarked. "Either they put his back up or he rubs them the wrong way, I'm never quite sure which."

Hobbs made no comment.

"All right, he can go." Gideon agreed. "I'll have a word with him first, though."

"I'll send for him," promised Hobbs. "The other case is out at Richmond. A thirteen-year old girl has disappeared."

Gideon's heart dropped; if there was one kind of crime he hated above all it was an offence against a young girl.

"Since when?"

"She should have been home at half-past seven last night, and at nine o'clock the father reported her missing. She'd been home to tea and gone back to school to play tennis. She didn't stay long with the girls she played with, but went off on her own."

"Anything known?" asked Gideon.

"There have been some complaints

about young girls being molested in Richmond Park, but nothing very serious," Hobbs answered.

"Did you talk to Hellier?"

"Yes. He's asked the adjoining divisions for help, and would like assistance from us."

"Does he want the river dragged?"

"He appears to think it might be too soon for that," Hobbs said, making it clear that he had asked the Divisional Superintendent about dragging. "I've had a word with the Thames Division at Barnes, to alert them."

"Good," Gideon said. "They can have all the help they want." He took more reports from Hobbs and spread them over his desk, making it look much more familiar, then glanced up. "Did you ask how Hellier is going about it?"

"He's using a hundred men in groups of twenty-five. One group's at the river, one checking the neighbours, one checking the school and the girls the child was playing with, one in the park. They're examining all newly-dug soil and any turf which seems to have been disturbed recently."

"All right, all right," Gideon interrupted. "I shouldn't have asked." He turned back to the files. "What about the Hendon bank robbery?"

"No news."

"The Fulham smash and grab?"

"The injured jeweller isn't as badly hurt as it was first suggested. We've found fingerprints on a patch of smooth cement on the brick, but they're not in *Records*."

"Hm." Gideon thumbed through the remaining reports; on those where there was nothing new Hobbs had clipped a duplicated *Nothing to report* on the top document. "Send Micklewright in, will you?"

"At once," said Hobbs.

He went out of the door from which he had come, and as it closed behind him Gideon heard a murmur of voices. Almost at once there was a tap, and on Gideon's "come in" a tall, sandy-haired, freckle-faced man entered, all arms and legs and hands and feet; Gideon never saw Micklewright without thinking of a music hall comedian. He realised that Hobbs had anticipated whom he would send to the airport and also that he, Gideon, would want a word with him.

"Sit down, Mick," Gideon said, and in a fluster of movement Micklewright obeyed, sitting on the edge of a straight-backed chair and crossing his legs; his right knee seemed to make a football in his trousers. "How's Clara?"

"She's fine sir, just fine." Micklewright's voice was pitched somewhat high.

"Good. Do you know Inspector Van Hoorn?"

"I couldn't say I know him," answered Micklewright, "but I know the man by sight and to talk to."

"He speaks good English, doesn't he?"

"Aye, when he's a mind to."

"Mick," Gideon said, "we had three letters of complaint from Oslo after you'd been over there on the Vigler jewel job, and they're not as touchy as the Dutch."

"They didna know a thing about jewels, mind."

"Van Hoorn probably knows more than you about diamonds."

Micklewright stopped fidgeting and, as a result, seemed to be uncannily still.

"That I take leave to doubt," he said, precisely.

Gideon grinned. "Prove how much you

know then, and don't rub him up the wrong way. And Mick—"

"Yes, sir?"

"I don't want any more complaints. Lay off the Scotch."

"I'll behave," Micklewright said with a rather sad smile. "Don't worry, sir, don't worry at all."

But in his way, Gideon did worry, for Micklewright had only recently started to drink much. Irascible at the best of times, never able to suffer fools gladly, some new influence was making him very edgy these days. Domestic affairs? wondered Gideon. He had an attractive wife but she was surely too old to be—

Gideon's train of thought was cut short when one of his telephones rang; the one from the Yard's exchange. The door closed on Micklewright as he lifted the receiver.

"Gideon."

"Mr. Worby, sir, of Thames."

"Put him through . . . Hello, Warbler," Gideon used an old nickname without thinking—"haven't heard from you since the Centenary Dinner. How are you?" There followed rather more small talk than usual with Gideon, for this was an old friend, but at last he said: "What can I do for you?"

Chief Superintendent Worby of Thames Division had a half-jocular manner of talking, as if even he was serious he wanted to kid whoever was at the other end of the line.

"Ever heard of industrial diamonds, George?"

Gideon's expression hardened but his voice was quite controlled.

"What about them?"

"A little bird tells me Amsterdam is worried about some going astray."

"I don't know any Dutch bird," Gideon said, still flat-voiced."

Worby chuckled.

"Tell you what's happened, George. We've a lot of trouble with your land boys, always doing their job for them, and last night we helped them to pick up a local would-be gangster who was terrifying the life out of his girl friend and her new boy friend. The pair took refuge in a boat. The would-be gangster pitched a couple of barrels on to them, hoping to sink the boat. He didn't, lucky for him, or he'd be on a murder charge. But my boys keep their eyes peeled, George, and they went to the scene of the crime this morning. Lodged on a pile of drift-wood they found a waterproof packet. Guess what was in it."

"Was it big enough for a packet of diamonds?" asked Gideon, and pressed a bell under his desk.

"It was. About two thousand quid's worth, I'd say."

Hobbs came in.

"Send it up to Waterloo Pier right away," Gideon said into the telephone. "We'll have a man waiting to pick it up. Hold on . . . Alec, get Micklewright back, don't let him leave the building. Tell him a packet of industrial diamonds was found in the river this morning and they'll be at the Thames Division station at Waterloo Pier in about half-an-hour's time. He can examine it on his way to see Van Hoorn."

Hobbs said: "Yes, at once," and went out.

"Still there, Warbler?" asked Gideon.

"I've laid that on," Worby told him. "The packet will be there in twenty minutes or so. Nice timing, was it, George?"

"Very nice timing," Gideon approved. "Thanks. Where do you think the packet came from—one of the barrels?"

"Could have been, but it would only be a guess. I've got the barrels in for inspection."

"Good," said Gideon, "I'll call you later."

That was the very moment when Wanda Pierce, whose daughter had been missing for nearly eighteen hours now, was saying in a weary voice:

"Only three days before her birthday. Oh, what an awful time for anything like this to happen. What an awful time."

Her husband took her hand gently, very gently.

"She'll come back," he made himself say. "She'll come back in time for her birthday. You needn't worry."

"Of course I worry!" the woman cried, snatching her hand free. "How do you know she'll come back? How do you know she hasn't been killed? Go on—tell me! How do you *know*?"

Chapter Three

ANGUISH

David Pierce felt his wife's fingers biting into his forearm, saw the glassy brightness of her eyes—usually a beautiful blue, like Geraldine's. Oh, God, like Geraldine's. She had not slept all night but he had dozed once or twice during that awful waiting, after the police had almost carried him home at the end of the first day's search.

Everything—everything hurt so much.

The dread in her eyes; the tautness at her lips; the pallor of her cheeks; the weight in his chest, as if it were forcing his heart down to his bowels. The sheer physical anguish of it all was almost unbearable; how could fear be so physical, send such pain through his body, his arms, his legs, make him feel sick with nausea? The shrillness of Wanda's voice hurt, too.

"... How do you know she hasn't been killed? Go on—Tell me! How do you *know*?"

He did not know.

He feared what Wanda feared, that their beloved Dina, their only child, had been lured away by some maniac, who—

But he must pretend for Wanda's sake.

"*Tell me!*" Wanda screamed.

"I just feel it in my bones," said David Pierce, flatly. "I just don't believe anything has happened to her."

"Of course it has, she's *dead*. Some devil attacked her and—oh dear God, what's happened to my Dina? What's *happened* to her?" Tears filled the woman's eyes although she had cried so much it seemed there could be no tears left. "Those little beasts who call themselves her friends shouldn't have let her go off alone. That's the truth—she would have been all right with them. It's *their* fault." The tears were dried up in sudden fury. "I'm going to see those mothers, I'm going to tell them its *their* fault, if they'd brought their children up properly—"

"Wanda, please—"

"I'm going, I tell you! How would they like it if this had happened to their child? Don't try to stop me! I'm going." She thrust him aside with more strength than he had expected, or known in her before, and sent him staggering. He was so helpless, and she—she looked so like Dina. The same dark hair cut just above the neck, the same slender hips, the same free, swinging movement.

A policeman appeared from the kitchen, where he had been for some time. Big and solid, he blocked the doorway. A cup of tea steamed in his hand.

"Thought you might like a cuppa," he said affably. "Don't mind me finding my way about your kitchen, I hope." He drew the cup back quickly as Wanda Pierce struck at him, and tea slopped into the saucer. "Take sugar, do you?"

"*Get out of my way!*" screamed Wanda.

"Oh. Sorry, ma'am." The policeman, round-faced and still affable, drew to one side in the narrow passage, and Wanda pushed past him, rushing towards the front door. She snatched at the handle, as the policeman dropped the saucer. It broke with a noise like a shot, and Wanda swung round, in shocked alarm. The policeman stood there stupidly, cup in hand.

"You clumsy fool!" Wanda cried. "Look

what you've done." She stood at the closed door, hands clenched and raised. David moved uncertainly towards her, not knowing what to do, hardly recognising his wife of fifteen years. Suddenly, she collapsed against him, sobbing, and in her anguish there was a momentary easement of his own. He led her back to the dining-room and as she passed the policeman, the man winked. He had dropped the saucer deliberately to distract Wanda.

A ring at the front door was almost a relief—and then, suddenly, a cause of tension: this could be *news*. Wanda's body went rigid.

"I'll go," offered the policeman. A moment later, his voice changed. "Good morning, doctor!"

Doctor? They had sent for no doctor.

There was a murmur of voices before short, dapper, young-looking Dr. Wade came in, brisk and forthright.

"Good morning, Mrs. Pierce," he said as Wanda freed herself and stared at him. He nodded to David. "I think it's time—"

Wanda cried: "Is there any news of my daughter?"

"Everything possible is being done to

find her," Dr. Wade said in a matter-of-fact tone. "She probably ran away in a fit of temper. You know, Mrs. Pierce, you aren't going to be able to help if you don't have some rest."

"*Rest*! How on earth *can* I rest, when I don't know where Dina is? When I don't know—"

"Mrs. Pierce," Dr. Wade interrupted sharply, "when Geraldine gets back she will need your help. If you're in hysterics, you'll only make her feel worse. Now I'm going to give you an injection. You won't feel it, and it won't make you sleep too long. Just hold out your left arm."

"I—I don't want an injection!"

Dr. Wade looked into David Pierce's eyes and took a small box out of his pocket. David gripped his wife's hand and pushed her left sleeve back above the elbow, and as Wanda stiffened in stubborn resistance, he held her tightly. Wade rubbed a spot on her arm with a piece of cotton wool, pinched the flesh, and put the needle in, all very swiftly.

"I don't want an injection!" repeated Wanda, but she didn't pull herself free.

"You need some tea or coffee with a lot

of sugar," Wade said, briskly. "And I'll see Geraldine the moment she's found. That's a promise."

"Promise!" Wanda echoed, stupidly. "Promise!"

"Hold her!" Dr. Wade said sharply.

David Pierce felt her dead weight fall against his body. Almost at once he saw Mrs. Edmond, a neighbour from across the street, and another woman whose name he did not know just behind her.

"We'll take her upstairs," said Mrs. Edmond, also matter-of-factly.

"Like me to carry her?" asked the policeman. Without waiting for a reply, he lifted the unconscious woman, and carried her from the room with no apparent effort, followed by the two visitors.

David Pierce watched them disappear up the narrow staircase then turned back to the dining-room and stood by the closed french windows, which opened on to a small garden with a patch of grass bright and trim, some roses, and a bed of multi-coloured antirrhinums, as fine as any he had ever grown. His expression was one of bleak despair. There were movements above his head as the neighbours busied themselves: and Wanda had never had much to do with neighbours, but how lost they would be without them, now.

"You could do with some rest, too," Dr. Wade told him.

"I'm all right," muttered Pierce. "If Wanda's all right, I am." He broke off, "I'd better telephone the office, as soon as I can. My—my boss won't like me being late."

"He won't mind at a time like this, surely."

"He's—he's a funny chap. I must telephone." Pierce closed his eyes. "Doctor—*is* there any news?"

"Not yet, I'm afraid," Wade said, gently.

"What—what do the police really think?"

"They're doing everything they can to trace her, you can be sure of that." Wade tried to be reassuring, just as David Pierce had tried to be with Wanda, and his words sounded just as empty. "Have you a telephone?"

"No. There's one in the High Street, though."

"Mrs. Edmonds has one," said Dr. Wade. "I'm sure she would like you to call from there."

"Really, Pierce, you know how busy we are," said Edward Lee, Pierce's employer. "Yes, of course it's worrying but you don't know that anything's happened to her yet . . . Come in as soon as you can, we must get the Seaborne analysis finished this week . . . I shall expect you to work late, of course . . ."

That was the time when David Carter and Samuel Cottingham were standing in the dock at Greenwich Police Court and Chief Inspector Singleton was giving evidence of arrest.

The magistrate was a very big, very deliberate man.

"And have the accused anything to say ?" he asked.

"Not guilty," Dave Carter said quickly. He was surprisingly small, very wiry-looking and had a suspicion of a hare-lip. "It was just a lark, sir, that's all."

"That's right," said Cottingham, whose hair was as long as a girl's and whose nose was almost as pointed as Cyrano de Bergerac's. "Not guilty, me lord."

"What do the police ask for ?"

"A remand in custody while inquiries

are being made, sir," Singleton said.

"Custody?" queried the magistrate.

A youthful, shiny-faced man stood up at the back of the court.

"I'll put up surety, in any reasonable amount, sir," he announced.

"For both the accused?"

"Yes, sir, if it's not too high."

In the well of the court, Mary Rose and Tom Argyle-Morris sat close together, almost as frightened as they had been the previous night.

"What do you say about bail?" the magistrate asked Singleton.

"We oppose it, sir, having reason to believe that the two witnesses might be menaced by the accused." Singleton spoke without any expression or apparent feeling.

"Why that's crazy!" cried Dave Carter. "It was only a lark, I tell you!"

The magistrate looked at him levelly. "A very unfortunate lark, I must say. I shall remand you both in custody for eight days."

Carter caught his breath. Cottingham rubbed his nose. The shiny-faced man muttered, audibly: "That's persecution, that is." Quite clearly, Carter said:

"Flicking bastard," but the magistrate and his clerk pretended not to hear.

Both Mary Rose and Tom looked noticeably relieved as they left the court. Singleton left just after them, satisfied, but preoccupied about the packet of industrial diamonds found in the water at Fiddler's Steps.

Detective Superintendent Micklewright waited as the KLM twin-engined jet taxied towards the entrance to the Customs shed at Heathrow. The Customs men knew him well; it was surprising how often he came here over smuggling and theft investigation. He saw two nice-looking women, a girl and several business men come out, followed by Van Hoorn. The Dutchman had the widest pair of shoulders Micklewright had ever seen on a man; he was only about five feet seven and that made his breadth of shoulder even more noticeable. He carried a small shiny black attaché case.

"Looks like a bloody hangman," Micklewright muttered under his breath, then beamed and went forward, splay-footed, big hand outstretched, feeling as if

Gideon's hand were on his shoulder. "Good morning, Inspector, very glad to see you again . . . We needn't bother with Customs, we trust all policemen!" He led the way through a side door and out to the front of the terminal building, where his car and driver were waiting.

"You are very kind," Van Hoorn said stiffly.

"Pleasure, Inspector, pleasure." Micklewright started to slam the door, saw Van Hoorn's thick fingers on the frame and snatched his hand away. The driver was there to close the door, anyhow. He walked round the back of the car and got in the other side, kicking against Van Hoorn's foot as he sat down. "Sorry. Have a good flight?"

"It was uneventful," stated Van Hoorn. His voice was slightly guttural, and yet high-pitched at the same time. "I studied all the documents, and depositions of the man we caught. I hope you will agree there is much evidence that the stolen jewels do come to England."

"Wouldn't be at all surprised," said Micklewright, opening his own battered pigskin brief-case. "We had a bit of luck last night. Quite fortuitous," he added slyly, but Van Hoorn gave no sign that the word puzzled him. Micklewright took out the waterproof packet, now unsealed, and held it towards the Dutchman. "Is this one of the Dutch consignments?"

Van Hoorn's slatey grey eyes shone suddenly with excitement; the expression put life into his face, and he seized the package.

Something outside the car caught Micklewright's eye—an airport policeman, waving. Just beyond this man was a woman and on that instant Micklewright thought it was his wife. His heart seemed to expand, then slowly, very slowly, to shrink. It wasn't Clara; it couldn't be Clara. The woman just happened to have Clara's attractive kind of grey hair with a slightly blue tint, and a black and white check suit, like Clara's; and she had an absurdly small waist—Clara's waist.

She passed.

Micklewright rubbed his sweaty hands together, and stared in the other direction oblivious of the rustling of the polythene bag which Van Hoorn was easing out of its outer waterproof container, and of the curious whistling sound which Van Hoorn made as he took a fold of linen from the bag. He opened this and peered down at the scintillating diamond chips which were fastened to the linen's wash-leather lining by strips of transparent plastic.

"Yes," he breathed. "This is one of the missing consignments. The inside packing is exactly the same. You will see." He opened his case and took out a folded pad exactly like the one found in the Thames. "There can be no mistake. This is good very good." He almost dropped the 'y' in 'very', almost added a 't' after good. "Where did you find it?"

Micklewright was staring out of the window, chin thrust forward, eyes narrowed, lips set tightly, his hands spread over his knees like an octopus with its tentacles tightening round a victim. Van Hoorn raised his eyebrows and fell silent. They crawled out of the parking area and were soon on the underpass and out on the main highway. Van Hoorn continued to inspect the diamonds on the two pads, as if trying to see any dissimilarities.

Micklewright turned his head, as if with an effort.

"Er—sorry," he said. "You said something." The weight lifted and he went on in a stronger voice. "Oh, yes, the industrial sparklers. Is it one of your consignments?"

"I am quite sure that it is," replied Van Hoorn, patiently. "This is a big step forward. May I ask you where it was found?"

"A big slice of luck," Micklewright said, and explained in detail. "It may have been in one of those barrels but more likely it was dropped or thrown overboard from a ship. No use guessing. We'll cover all the possibilities as soon as we can." By the time he finished, they were moving fast along the Great West Road. "I've told the Thames Division to lay on some lunch for us, and we can have a look round from there. And I've told the Port of London Authority chaps to expect us this afternoon sometime. Tell you one thing, though. If the crooks are bringing the stuff in by the river—or taking it out by the river if it comes to that—what price the man you caught who flies between here and Amsterdam so often?"

"It is one of the problems we have to discuss," Van Hoorn said stiffly. The sympathy he had felt for the Scotland Yard man because of his obvious troubles, dried up. Micklewright had a reputation in Amsterdam, Brussels, Paris—in fact in most of the European capitals—for being far too insular, a difficult man to work with and one who was always trying to score off continental detectives. Now he was virtually telling him, Van Hoorn, that the Dutch police had made a mistake over the suspect who had been arrested in Holland. Van Hoorn geared himself for a difficult time.

Chapter Four

GIDEON WALKS

No one knew about the cave in the old quarry except the man who had discovered it, several years before and who had made his home there. To reach it, he had to climb down one shallow side of the quarry and cross ten yards or more of water; this water was several feet deep, except in the middle where an earth fall had made a kind of bridge; even after heavy rain the water there never rose higher than his ankles, and he always wore boots which came halfway up his calves. He had furnished this home gradually, piece by piece, from furniture found on rubbish dumps. In a recess there was an old oilstove, a frying pan, a kettle and a saucepan, and he always kept a bucket of rainwater there. Near the stretch of water opposite the cave was an old shed, once used for tools, but now empty and derelict. Rainwater dripped off the corrugated iron roof into an old drum, from which he refilled his bucket.

Very few people ever came near, and when they did, they could not see the cave, which was hidden by a jutting piece of sandstone, Behind this, and across the mouth of the cave he had built a ramshackle wooden wall, with a tiny window and a door which he could bolt from the inside. This gave him a sense of protection and security.

Jonathan Jones—for such was the man's name—was gearing himself for a difficult time; as Van Hoorn had done. He sat in a rocking chair, lurching gently to and fro, to and fro. On the one narrow bed, in a corner and beneath the hole which served as a window, lay a girl, asleep.

She was a pretty child, with full lips and a snub nose. She had dark, bobbed hair and, even as she lay, her figure appeared more a woman's than a girl's. She had a tiny waist, drawn in tightly, a dark red skirt and a grubby white blouse. She appeared to be sleeping quite naturally.

Now and again Jones shook his head.

Suddenly, he leaned forward and stretched out his right hand, touching the child's ankle; his touch was still light as he ran his hand up and down the calf of her leg. She wore no stockings, and her skin was enticingly soft. He rocked and stroked, rocked and stroked. The chair made a slight creaking noise, the only sound.

His difficulty was to decide what to do with her.

She was nice; very nice.

He hadn't frightened her; not really.

But when she woke she would remember and when she remembered she would want to scream, and if she got away it would not be long before the police arrived.

It was a very, very difficult time. He had to decide what to do, soon. He did not know how long she would sleep, but it would not be for more than two or three hours. That wasn't very much time in which to make such a decision. He did not want to kill her but on the other hand he did not want to be caught by the police. If he were caught he would be sent to prison, and goodness knew what would happen to him there.

It would really be better if the girl did not wake; it would solve so many of his problems.

To and fro, he went: to and fro.

Up and down went his hand over the satiny skin: up and down.

Gideon heard a man laughing.

It was a pleasant laugh, perhaps little more than a chuckle, as if the other were deeply amused, and hearing it, Gideon's pre-occupations faded. He was in St. James's Park, watching the lake, the wild ducks so nearly tame, the masses of flowers, the people sauntering over grass and along the paths. A thicket of bushes hid him from the man, but a few yards further along he saw what was happening. A child of four or five was trying to stand on his head. Up he would go, legs waving wildly, scarlet in the face, supporting himself with his hands; then over he would tumble, only to be up again on the instant game for another try. He wore very short blue shorts and a singlet. The man, wearing a short-sleeved shirt of pale blue, looked spruce and scrubbed. Neither child nor man said a word. The child tried twice again, so intent and so earnest that Gideon also began to smile.

Then as the child thumped down with the inevitable tumble, the man said: "That's enough, kiddo." As the boy started again he moved forward, grabbed and swung the lad over his head. Now it was the boy's turn to chuckle. Gideon started to move on; he hadn't been noticed yet, and there was something curiously private and personal about the little scene.

Swinging the child to the ground, however, the man turned and came almost face to face with him. On that instant his expression changed, he lowered his arms quickly but in full control.

Gideon had a shock: for the last time he had seen this man, he had been in the dock in the Old Bailey; it must be seven or eight years ago.

"Hallo, Mr. Miller," he said. "Haven't seen you for a long time."

Miller stared, his face and body tensed; then, very slowly, he relaxed,

"No, we haven't met, have we?"

"Your son?" inquired Gideon.

"You could say so," Miller replied. There was a curious twist to his lips which puzzled Gideon for a moment; then the penny dropped and he was appalled by his own gaucheness. Miller had served six years at least, and the child could be no more than four or five.

Once again Miller gave that pleasant chuckle.

"Let's say, adopted son," he said. "I'll settle for that."

"Lively youngster," Gideon observed. "How long have you been back in London?"

"Six months or so."

"Everything all right?"

"I've my own little haulage business, thanks to my wife," said Miller. "Yes, everything's fine, now." His eyes filled with laughter and it came to Gideon that he was a happy man. "How are tricks in your line of business?"

"Too many for my liking," Gideon said.

"Daddy—" the child began, its patience wilting.

"Okay, kiddo, we'll go and look at the ducks. Good day, Mr. Gideon." He took the child's hand.

Gideon nodded and passed on, his thoughts carrying him back over the years. Miller had been a cashier for one of the big Joint Stock banks, and had helped thieves to break into a suburban branch where he had once worked. Now he had a haulage business, "thanks to my wife". What exactly had that meant?

Gideon, already later than he had intended, stepped out more briskly.

He was due for a conference at Savile Row Police Station with two divisional men and an insurance broker. There had been a lot of fur robberies in recent months, mostly in Mayfair, and the police had been too long a time without making an arrest. The conference could easily have taken place at the Yard but then three men would have had to travel, and Gideon wasn't under any particular pressure that afternoon, moreover the walk through the park, then past Clarence House, up to St. James's Palace, across Piccadilly and along Bond Street to Savile Row, had attracted him. This was part of his old "manor", his square mile; seeing it now filled him with nostalgia—in a way, the encounter with Miller had done the same thing.

He turned into Savile Row Police Station five minutes late, at twenty past three. Almost immediately a sergeant accosted him.

"Excuse me, Commander."

"Yes?"

"You're asked to contact your office at once, sir."

"Right, thanks," Gideon said. "Where's the nearest phone?"

"As a matter of fact, sir, I saw you pass the window, the Yard's on the line now."

"Thanks." Gideon glanced keenly at the sergeant, an eager-faced man in his thirties obviously out to make a good impression. Well, he had.

The telephone was in the charge room, and as Gideon lifted the receiver he heard Hobbs' voice. "*Is* Mr. Gideon there?"

"Yes," Gideon said. "What's on?"

"Hellier wants to use frogmen to drag the river for the Pierce girl," Hobbs told him, almost too abruptly. "Her school satchel was found washed up on the bank near Teddington weir."

Gideon pondered, his spirits suddenly cast down.

Hobbs would have given authority had he felt it justified; the very fact that he raised the query meant that he was doubtful. And he was right to be doubtful. Once frogmen were used the case would become a major newspaper sensation, and that would tear the hearts out of the parents and could put ideas into the heads of men already teetering on the brink of that half-world of lust and lunacy which made them long sexually for a little girl. If one traced the incidents of this kind of crime, one found that they came in cycles. There might be months without a single one, then a sensational case, and half-a-dozen would follow.

Gideon pulled himself up short; there was no certainty, yet, that a crime had been committed.

"No," he said. "Only if Hellier's virtually certain he'll find the body in the river."

"I'll see to it," said Hobbs.

Gideon rang off, the sergeant with his eye on the main chance was entering notes in the duty ledger. As Gideon nodded to him and went out, a neatly-dressed, nicely made-up young woman came in, nervousness and anxiety clear on her face.

"Good afternoon, Madam."

"I'm sorry to trouble you but I *think* someone's broken into my house . . . "

So it went on, day in, day out, crime following crime in a shapeless pattern, playing on human fears and emotions, harassing and harrowing. It had given Gideon his livelihood, he was dedicated to its service; but *why* did it happen with such remorseless, unending regularity?

The two divisional men and the insurance broker were waiting in a smoke-filled office overlooking the street, and a fur salon with a single sable on display was immediately across the road. The broker was Jewish, bright-eyed and alert, with a soft, attractive voice; the two senior policemen obviously had a great respect for him. They were big men of the same type, difficult to distinguish one from the other.

"Very glad to meet you, Commander . . . As I've told these gentlemen, nine out of eleven fur robberies in the West End area in the past three months have been from stores whose insurance goes through my hands. If it happens much more I shan't get any business, everyone will think I'm responsible."

"Are you?" asked Gideon, with heavy humour.

"No, I am not, and it is no joking matter," said the insurance broker. "But as many of the robberies take place when new stocks have just been delivered and in some cases are still in transit, I think it possible that a member of my staff might be involved. What I should like to do, sir, is to have one of your detectives on my staff for a while."

"A woman?" Gideon asked.

"Oh, a woman, of course."

"Be much less noticeable," The Divisional Superintendent remarked. "But it has to be someone knowledgeable about furs, and we haven't anyone here."

"I'll see what we can produce at the Yard," Gideon promised. "And we'll watch all the shops and the warehouses as new stocks go in and out. What's worrying you in particular, Mr. Morris?"

The broker leaned forward in his chair. "As a matter of fact, Commander, a very large collection of Russian sable and Russian and Canadian mink is due tomorrow. It's for a special mannequin parade to be held next Monday and Tuesday on the river between Chelsea and Tower Bridge. It's going to be a very big show, Commander."

"I hadn't heard of it," Gideon said, suddenly interested.

"It's been widely advertised by word of mouth in the trade and in society," said the broker, "but no one will know where it's to be held until the last minute. The furs will be transferred to the boat from Chelsea pier, I'm told." Morris was obviously taking this very seriously indeed. "I am responsible only for the insurance of the furs, but there will also be displays of jewellery, and of course the guests will be very wealthy people. I'm very troubled about it, Commander."

"Have we been officially notified?" Gideon demanded.

"Not to my knowledge, sir, but I am not the organiser."

"Who is?"

"Sir Jeremy Pilkington. He's hiring the *River Belle*, I believe, and several other boats besides. The proceeds will be for charity, Sir Jeremy is a very prominent gentleman in organising such affairs. One of the features of this one is the mystery—on the other hand, I feel so strongly that these furs should be *fully* protected that I felt I should tell you—in strict confidence, of course."

"Yes," Gideon said. "We appreciate it. Monday and Tuesday, you say?"

"Yes, in five days' time."

"We'll keep an eye on things," Gideon

promised, "and I'll see whom we can find to join your staff for a longer term purpose."

"I'm very grateful, Commander."

Gideon left the office just after four o'clock, this time stepping into a car which the Divisional men had laid on. Traffic was so thick that it took him almost as long to reach the Yard as if he had walked. He was very much more thoughtful, quite able to understand why Morris had preferred not to come to the Yard and realising that the implications of the insurance man's story could be very widespread. He turned into his own office and opened the door to Hobbs's.

Hobbs wasn't there.

Gideon went to his own desk and picked up the telephone.

"Get me Mr. Prescott, of AB Division," he ordered. "And when I'm finished get Mr. Worby of Thames." He put down the receiver, then lifted another telephone which was direct to *Information.* A man answered: "*Info*'."

"This is Commander Gideon," Gideon said heavily. "Is there any news from Richmond about the missing girl?"

"No, sir, nothing fresh. Mr. Hobbs was just inquiring about it."

"Is he still with you?"

"Left a minute ago, sir."

Gideon grunted and rang off as the other telephone rang.

"Mr. Prescott, sir."

"Good afternoon, Commander." Prescott was bright, brisk, breezy, a man in his middle fifties who never seemed to grow older.

"Hallo, Lance. Have you had any request for special parking near Chelsea Bridge next week?"

"No? Should I have?"

"I wouldn't be surprised. Has Lex, do you know?"

Lex was the Superintendent in charge of ST Division, which controlled the riverbank on the Surrey side.

"Nothing big, anyhow—I had lunch with him today, and he would have said if there had been."

"Thanks." Gideon rang off, pressed the bell for Hobbs, and stood up, going to the window and staring at the shimmering surface of the river. With the huge Shell buildings on the other side, as well as the

Festival Hall, the South Bank really had a massive and impressive skyline.

Hobbs came in, almost at once.

"You heard what Sir Jeremy Pilkington's up to?" asked Gideon abruptly.

Hobbs, unexpectedly, gave a quick smile. "Not lately!"

"Do you know him?"

"Yes. Not well, but I know him."

"According to some news I picked up—" Gideon broke off, leaned towards the telephone and lifted it, adding: "Listen to this . . . Hallo, Warbler . . . Anything from Micklewright and Van Hoorn? . . . Well, it can wait . . . Have you heard of a special river parade due to take place next week? Sir Jeremy Pilkington's said to have hired the *River Belle* and is having a flotilla or something between Chelsea and Tower Bridge? . . . Yes, I'll hold on." Gideon kept the receiver at his ear and spoke to Hobbs. "I got this from Morris, the insurance chap, he's worried about it. Hello? . . . Yes, Warbler . . . yes . . . let me make sure I have it straight. You've been told that the *River Belle* has been chartered for a special party and that there will be some small boats with her but you haven't been told what it's about. Right . . . Do the Port of London Authority know any more? . . . Find out, will you? . . . I'm checking but I think you may have to make special arrangements for those evenings. I'll let you know. Thanks."

He rang off, hardly aware that he had said so much in few words, and completely unaware of the fact that Hobbs was looking at him with a kind of amused admiration.

"We could be making a fuss about nothing," he remarked to Hobbs, "but I don't want to be caught napping. Can you find out unofficially what Pilkington has in mind?"

"Yes," Hobbs said promptly.

"Good. Things still quiet generally?"

"Fairly quiet," Hobbs answered. "It must be summer sloth!" He was beginning to show much more of his human side. "A nice time for a river trip," he added drily.

"Now what are you getting at?" Gideon asked.

"You mentioned a week or so ago that you hadn't been on the river for a year or more, and suddenly there's a crop of river investigations. It might be a good idea

if you had a day on the river tomorrow."
Hobbs was obviously serious.

Slowly, thoughtfully, Gideon remarked: "Not a bad idea at all. I might do it, if the weather's right." It passed through his mind that it was a long time since anyone at the Yard had suggested anything *he* should do, it was usually the other way round. Was it really possible that Hobbs was going to share his burden, the very real burden, of the Commander's job?"

It was a funny thought, which made Gideon feel a little rueful, even a little old. But it did not stop him from hoping that it would be a nice day tomorrow.

Chapter Five

NICE DAY

Gideon woke soon after seven o'clock the next morning, to bright sunlight. Kate, his wife, lying next to him, was also beginning to stir; suddenly her eyes opened and stayed open with that half puzzled, half comprehending expression which often comes on the moment of waking. Her eyes, even though her back was to the windows, were very clear, bright blue.

"Good morning, love."

"Hello, George," Kate said. "What's the weather like?"

"Sunny."

"The television said it would be," Kate said. She stretched, luxuriously, with a hint of sensuousness, and Gideon was acurely aware of her. Their bodies were close. "Didn't you say you might go on the river today?"

"Yes."

"I'm going over to see Pru," Kate said. "She might like a day by the river, too."

"I'll keep an eye open for you."

"I don't know that I like the idea of the police looking out for me." Kate gave a little smile which screwed her mouth up in a way which had attracted him for nearly thirty years. Quite suddenly, he kissed her; and for a few moments his arms were very tight around her. It *was* early. Gideon glanced at the window again—then heard a chink of cups at the door, breaking the spell.

"Anyone awake?" It was Malcolm, their youngest son, who was not usually up so early.

Gideon eased himself away from Kate and over on to his back.

"Come in, Malcolm."

The door turned, the youth entered with the tray balanced precariously on one hand; he was beaming, obviously very pleased with himself. At sixteen, he showed some signs of being as big as his father, but his features were narrower and more like Kate's.

"Just to show you that I *can* wake by myself," Malcolm said.

"Mal, be *careful*."

"Pooh, I won't drop it."

"Where are you going today?" demanded Gideon. "Not having a day by the river, too, are you?"

"No, worse luck. Victoria and Albert Museum. *Art*," added Malcolm with a grimace; he was the least artistic of all their children. "As a matter of fact I've got a game of tennis before school, I'll get my own brekker, Mum."

"Knew there was some reason for you waking up," Gideon remarked. His mood was so good that he had almost forgotten that he had been interrupted.

An hour later, bacon and eggs, coffee and toast inside him, he started off to the Yard, choosing to drive along by the Embankment. Traffic was already heavy, and diesel fumes from a petroleum carrier nearly choked him. Through the fumes he could see white smoke billowing majestically from the four chimneys of the Battersea Power Station. The sun, coming across the river but already fairly high, misted the graceful span of the Albert and the more prosaic stretch of Battersea Bridge. There was faint mist over the pleasure gardens, too.

As he passed the lorry he drove faster

until, at the new, square Millbank ministry building, he slowed down, affected as always by this view of London, the Houses of Parliament, the Abbey, the wide grandeur of Whitehall beyond Parliament Square. The same man who had taken his car yesterday sprang forward.

"Nice morning, sir. Just right for a day on the river."

Gideon looked at him sharply but forebore to ask whether the remark was a coincidence, or whether rumour had spread. If Hobbs had told Worby of Thames Division then it might well have leaked out and the whole of the Yard would know it now. It was still very much a village in these days of radio and swift communication. As he turned towards his office, Micklewright appeared.

" 'Morning, Commander."

" 'Morning. How are things?"

"Going very well, very well indeed," Micklewright reported. "Van Hoorn thinks we have a police force after all." He followed Gideon into his office. "There isn't much doubt that that package came from a ship fairly recently, although it *could* have been in one of the barrels

Carter and his friends pushed down Fiddler's Steps. In which case someone could have been planning to collect it from the barrel. Only certain thing is that it was meant to stay in the water—the waterproofing was perfect. Someone hides packets like it in the water, a colleague on land picks them up. Or *vice versa.*"

Gideon said: "Yes. It certainly looks like it. Any specific ideas?"

"I've asked the Warbler to let us have a crew to show us all the places where small packets could be hidden easily."

"H'mm," Gideon said. "Going on the river today?"

"Yes. Picked the right day for it, haven't I?"

Gideon frowned. "I'm not sure you should go, Mick," he said slowly. Pressing the bell for Hobbs, he watched Micklewright's face, realising that it made no difference at all to the man whether he had his day out or not. Hobbs came in. "Alec, the Superintendent was planning to go on the river with Van Hoorn today. Van Hoorn's known to Customs, to the P.L.A. people, and to anyone who uses the docks regularly; if they see him on the river they'll know we've special reason to search there and may guess that we've found the packet of diamonds. I think the search should be left to the Thames Division."

"So do I," said Hobbs.

Micklewright glanced from one to the other. "While Van Hoorn and I try the airport and the diamond merchants, as if we haven't a clue?" he suggested.

"That's what I think," said Gideon.

"You're absolutely right," said Micklewright. "Why don't I think the way you do? I'll tell you one thing. This job could be very big."

"How big?"

"Van Hoorn estimates that the diamonds stolen in the past year are worth considerably more than a hundred thousand pounds."

"Does he indeed," said Gideon. "How long is he staying?"

"As long as it seems worthwhile."

"Have him come here and see me to-morrow," Gideon said, adding without pause: "Might as well make it lunch—you come too, Mick."

"Be delighted!"

"Any other clues at all?"

"Not yet," Micklewright said. "It's early days, though."

When he had gone out, Gideon pondered for a few minutes. Micklewright's manner was brittle and bright, but even at this hour there was the smell of whisky on his breath. Preoccupation about this was driven from Gideon's mind as two telephones rang at once. Hobbs picked up one, Gideon the other.

"Deputy Commander speaking."

"This is Gideon."

"Commander," Hellier of Richmond said in an uncompromising way, "there's still no trace of Geraldine Pierce, and I really think it's time we searched the river. I don't want to be stubborn, but we shouldn't leave it too long."

"Get the Thames Division to start dragging," Gideon agreed. "I'll see you some time late this morning and if we have to call the frogmen out, we will then."

"Right!" Hellier was obviously satisfied. "Look forward to seeing you, sir. I'll tell you one thing we *did* find while we were looking for the kid."

"What?"

"Body of a day-old child, strangled

and buried in the park," Hellier said. "Some poor young bitch got herself in trouble."

There was no need for any special instructions about the murdered baby. Infanticide by half-demented mothers was not infrequent and, shocking though it was, sympathy for the mother was almost inevitable. Gideon rang off, again momentarily depressed. He told Hobbs what he had done, and in a few seconds was free from depression and looking forward to going on the river.

"Will you have the Superintendent's launch, or a patrol boat?" Hobbs asked.

"A patrol boat on its beat," Gideon decided. "Have 'em pick me up at Westminster Pier in half-an-hour."

"There's one waiting there for you," said Hobbs.

So the fact that he was going out on the Thames *was* known, and Hobbs and Worby had guessed he would prefer a patrol boat. Gideon made no comment, went through the other cases pending, and then found a coloured postcard from Algiers at the bottom of the pile. He picked it up, thinking: Scott-Marle's on holiday there. It was from Scott-Marle, and almost an unprecedented gesture from the Commissioner. Gideon felt a moment of pleasure, put the card down, and remarked:

"He'll be away for another two weeks."

"Yes," said Hobbs.

"Did you see Pilkington?"

"No, he's in Paris," Hobbs answered. "But I saw his wife. He *is* arranging a kind of gala mannequin parade on the river, between five o'clock and eight o'clock next Monday or Tuesday evening. He plans to have floats with top fashion models showing all kinds of clothes, jewellery and furs. It will be quite a sensation."

"So I imagine," Gideon grunted. "What's all the secrecy about? They usually like to get as much publicity as they can for this kind of stunt."

"They're planning a big campaign in the week-end papers and on television," answered Hobbs. "The proceeds are for a World Food Campaign. All the invitations have gone out, and the guests told to look for the time and venue in the newspapers. The press have been invited in strength, of course. No one knows exactly how it will be done, and the secrecy is intended to heighten the effect. It should be very effective, George. Pilkington is the brains behind it, and he's obviously put a lot of effort into the preparations. Some of the best designers, furriers and jewel-merchants will exhibit."

"If it hadn't been for Morris the first we'd have heard of it would have been Sunday," grumbled Gideon. "As it is, we'll have to put all the Divisions with waterfronts on special alert, and warn the City chaps and port of London and the Thames Division. They'll have a major job on their hands. I'll tell Worby when I see him; you see to the rest."

"I will. What is your feeling about letting our precautions be known?"

Gideon pursed his lips.

"Pity to spoil their surprise—if that's how they want to do it, it's up to them. We needn't talk about it. Just put out a special alert to the Divisions affected. Better cancel all leave except the usual holidays, and arrange for overtime where it might be necessary."

"I'll have a report ready by morning," Hobbs promised. "There is one particular thing, George."

"Yes?"

"I told Esmeralda—Lady Pilkington—that we took a dim view of the fact that we hadn't been warned, and that the least they could do was to see we have a few complimentary tickets. I thought perhaps you'd like to take Kate, and if Priscilla will accept an elderly escort, I'd be happy to take her."

Gideon warmed to him in a way he never had before.

"Kate will love it, and if Priscilla hasn't a passionate boy friend at the moment, she will, too." He glanced at his watch. "I'd better be off."

It was only a step to the pier at Westminster Bridge. The patrol boat was waiting with Old Man River Singleton and P.C. Addis standing by, and Sergeant Tidy at the helm. It was the crew which had saved Tom Argyle and his girl, and found the packet of diamonds, although Gideon did not know this; nor did he know that they had all volunteered for this special spell of duty. Stepping over the polished side, he moved to the centre of the boat. It was pleasantly warm in a hazy sun. Two pleasure boats and several river trip launches were hove-to, one of them already loading passengers. A man with a croaking voice kept calling out:

"*Tower Bridge—Pool-a-London—Bloody Tower—London Bridge, all for three bob. Tower Bridge — Pool-a-London — Bloody Tower—London Bridge, all for three bob.*" There was no variation in his tone or expression.

The youngest man in the police crew cast off.

Gideon settled down at the seat in the stern. Old Man River Singleton balanced himself evenly, looking at Gideon. The engine began to growl. They went slowly towards midstream before heading down river. For the first few minutes Gideon forgot practically everything—the coming water parade, the diamond thefts, the missing Pierce child, all the crime that was taking place in London, all those conditions which "invited" crime, everything but the sensuous pleasure of feeling the sun on his face and the gentle sway of the boat.

Geraldine Pierce also felt the sun on her face. And it fell on the head of the man who now had his back to her. She could not move, for she was tied to the bed; she could not shout, for she was gagged. She lay in a kind of stupor, conscious and terrified and yet numbed.

It was the first time in her life she had felt fear.

It was not fear of a repetition of what had happened soon after the man had brought her here, not fear of being ravished—it was fear of being killed. She did not know what was in his mind, but she was no fool. She read newspapers, and she knew that this man, with his gentle, almost soothing touch and his soft and rather pleasant voice, was frightened of the police.

He had given her milk and bread and butter, some ham and some cheese.

He had cut the cheese with a knife.

He kept the knife close at hand, kept touching it, and turning to look at her.

If only he would take the gag off, she could plead with him.

Wanda Pierce looked at the tall, square block of a man, Superintendent Hellier of the Divisional force which served

Richmond division. He towered over her. She did not think of it consciously, but there was something hard and ruthless about him; about his rather small eyes which seldom blinked, the stubby brown eyelashes, even the brickish colour of his skin. His cheek bones were prominent, his jaw very square, even the way his hair grew on his forehead gave a square, symmetrical effect; not at all rounded. He had a harsh penetrating voice.

"So there's no news," Wanda said, emptily.

"No, none. I'm sorry." That was almost perfunctory. "I have given instructions for dragging the river, Mrs. Pierce. If we find anything we will inform you."

Wanda's heart seemed to become a ball of lead.

"Commander Gideon, the head of the Criminal Investigation Department, is coming to visit the scene in person," Hellier went on. "That gives you some idea of the importance we are attaching to this sad affair."

Sad—*Sad?* Dear God, it was agonising!

"Thank you," Wanda said stiffly.

The neighbour with her, plump and

fluffy Mrs. Edmond, said almost in despair:

"I'm sure she'll be all right, Wanda dear, I'm *sure* she will be."

Hellier thought bleakly: She hasn't got a chance. We'll find the body in the river. He did not say this, but something in his manner conveyed that impression. He turned and went out, and as the front door closed he heard the neighbour exclaim:

"What a brute of a man! He shouldn't be in the police."

The friendly policeman who had shown so much sympathy and understanding, was at the door. He must have heard the comment but made no sign.

Chapter Six

HARD SHELL

Dick Hellier got into his car outside the Pierces' home. His movements were always brisk but deliberate, almost as if he controlled the reflexes of his body as he controlled—or tried to control—the reactions of his mind. He sat back in the car and said to the driver:

"River."

"Yes, sir."

As the car moved off, two reporters drew near and a photographer leant down and took a photograph through the car window. Hellier was acutely aware of the fact that they hadn't approached him closely until he had settled into the car. They had just watched, blank-faced, almost sullen. They disliked and resented him, of course; in a way, they feared him. He knew that, just as he knew that the way he had talked to Mrs. Pierce had seemed harsh and unfeeling to her and her neighbour.

"What a brute of a man! He shouldn't be in the police."

And Constable Luckley had heard, of course; Luckley probably agreed.

Hellier, son of a Swedish sailor and an English mother who had been killed in the late stages of the bombing of London in 1944, did not understand why he felt as he did at this moment; almost savagely resentful. He had not meant to sound cold and indifferent, he had formed his words carefully so as to create a different impression, but he had failed. He always failed in his relationship with people, he thought bitterly. There was some quality missing in him.

When he had first heard of this case he had felt furiously angry, and determined at all costs to find both man and girl. Deep down inside him, only half-admitted, there was a special reason.

He knew the child, as he knew the mother; by sight.

Each had a quality which was rare, a quality he knew about vicariously but which he had not experienced personally for nearly twenty years. They had a sexual attractiveness, the kind of attractiveness which made them natural seductresses. He did not think the mother was aware of this quality in herself, and that might mean that she was unaware of it in her daughter. Hellier found it very hard to describe. It was far above anything which made youths turn their heads and whistle. It was not simply the fact that men would notice their slender legs and their slim hips. It was not their faces, attractive and alike though they were, nor their figures. It was something in the way they stood, walked, glanced about them; a kind of regality, an assurance of their own ascendancy.

Nonsense?

Hellier, groping for words as he sat still and outwardly morose in the back of the car, didn't think so.

The girl hadn't quarrelled with her three school friends. Why then, had she left them early? Why had she taken the long way home, by the river? Because, thought Hellier, she had known that along the river she would find youths and young men loitering and would revel in the effect she had on them. He suspected that the other girls had let her go alone because they knew that she would attract all the attention.

They, and their mothers, had virtually told him as much when he had questioned them.

And so Geraldine had gone off on her own.

And someone—

Some brute of a man!

Hellier drew in a sharp, hissing breath.

For a reason he could not understand, the thought and the momentary hurt drew him out of this mood of introspection and he became what he appeared to be to most people who knew him; a calculating machine, weighing up facts and drawing conclusions. He had one invaluable asset as a detective—a memory for names and faces, as well as for details of everyone he knew. He was a kind of walking records office where this Division was concerned.

An instance of his gift came at that moment, when a black Jaguar swept round a corner leading from the river. At the wheel was an austere, very handsome woman; Hellier, although he did not know her, recognised her immediately as a Mrs. Tollifer, from Rivers Meet. She and her husband lived in some style in a house with grounds which ran down to the river. Tollifer, a stockbroker, was reputed to be several times a millionaire, a big, genial, fleshy man. His wife appeared as cold as he, Hellier, was thought to be. For the first time Hellier wondered whether she was as frigid as she looked on the surface.

On the next corner, a milk dray was parked, safely tucked in but seemingly deserted; milk, cream, eggs and orange drink bathed in the afternoon sun. The milkman was Constantin Duros, a remarkable name for a milkman; he was a Greek, with a roving eye and a caressing voice and an indisputable attraction for his housewife customers. It was not unusual for this dray to be parked for half an hour or more, while Constantin Duros was nowhere to be seen.

"Don't know how he does it," Hellier's chief assistant had a habit of saying. "Three times a day sometimes and he must be over fifty!"

Coming along the street on his bicycle was "Daddy" Paterson, the postman, also in his fifties, with iron grey hair, iron grey eyes, a stalwart of the local council, a man who never wasted a word, was involved with nearly every do-gooding organisation in the district, and who had never looked at any woman since his wife had died seven years previously.

Hellier could place and catalogue an incredible number of people in his manor, their weaknesses, their idiosyncrasies, their likes and dislikes, even their potential for good or bad. This served him in remarkable stead in his job, which was in some ways the best organised division in the Metropolitan area, with a much higher ratio of solved cases than in most. This part of Richmond, of course, did not lend itself to much professional crime, but there was some: and pocket-picking, shop-lifting and car stealing was as rife here as in most Greater London areas.

He reached the pier at Barnes, where Gideon would come ashore, ten minutes before Gideon's patrol boat arrived. Several reporters had wind of who was coming, and stood close by. So did the Thames Division men, with whom Hellier worked closely. They got along well enough, for Hellier's efficiency was respected by everyone and personalities counted for very little. He stood talking to the Chief Inspector in charge of Barnes as the boat came chugging round the wide bend in the river.

Someone said: "There's Gideon—standing up."

The big man seemed to dominate not only the boat but the smooth expanse of river. In the other direction three patrol boats were dragging, systematically, and crowds lined the banks to watch. Several pleasure boats were moored close inshore, crowded with passengers watching this search for the body of a child.

"Lot of ghouls," stated Old Man River Singleton roundly. "I'd send the blighters packing if I had my way."

Gideon, standing while the other man now sat, nodded and said tritely: "Takes all sorts."

Gideon watched as the patrol boats gently moved, all going up river, all with the drags out. Unless it were weighted down, a body would float and be caught. Usually, he knew, it was possible to recognise that it *was* a body, but sometimes it floated too far beneath the surface for there to be any indication. There was a matter-of-fact air about all the men involved, those on the banks as well as those in the boats.

This one drew alongside with hardly a jolt. Gideon climbed out, the Thames man, Chief Inspector Bill Bell, shook hands.

"Glad to see you here, Commander."

"Haven't seen you for years," Gideon remarked, and was slightly vexed with himself; everything he said today seemed trite. It wasn't exactly an inspection, but even the river men, with their reefer jackets and curious air of informality, were on their best behaviour. "Any sign of the child?"

"No, sir." Bell looked like a sailor, even to the faraway expression in his eyes.

Gideon saw Hellier, who was standing on one side, nodded, but didn't go towards him at first. Bill Bell, a little self-conscious, glanced up river, and his expression changed.

"They've got something!" he exclaimed.

Every man on the pier and in the boats, every newspaper man, everyone in sight, spun round and stared at the middle one of the three boats which were dragging. One man was standing up with the hitching pole ready: something heavy was caught in the drag. The man with the hitching pole leaned forward and pulled gently. A camera clicked. Gideon took a swift look round and noticed Hellier's set profile, the thrust-forward chin, the obvious tension in his body.

Someone on the bank cried:

"They've got her!"

A woman turned away from a little group and scurried off, mounted a bicycle and raced along the path. Everyone in the pleasure boats craned their necks, a dozen cameras pointed at the swirl of water around the drag. Another police boat drew nearer. A man close to the rail of one pleasure boat suddenly retched and was sick. Gideon, forcing himself to study the policemen near him, read compassion and sadness in Singleton, a tight-lipped distaste in Sergeant Tidy, matter-of-factness in most of the others. Young Addis, the youngest member of the crew of his boat, said *sotto voce*:

"I'll never learn to like it."

Hellier stood like a rock; a man *made* of rock. Heartless? Gideon did not know him well, and liked little of what he did know, his main interest being in the fact that Hellier was one of the best detectives in the Force.

Someone cried shrilly: "It's only a dog!"

One of the men on the nearer boat nodded his head and relaxed. In a few moments the body of a big dog appeared clearly above the water. Orders were shouted, and one man called: "Bring it in." Someone gave a high-pitched laugh; a siren blasted, a bicycle bell tinkled.

"Anyone would think it was something to celebrate," grunted Singleton. "Haven't found the kid yet, then."

Gideon said to Hellier: "Do you still want those frogmen?"

Hellier turned, and seemed startled, as if he had been shaken out of a coma.

"Er—yes. Yes, sir. If you please."

Gideon turned to Singleton. "Will you fix the frogman team, Superintendent? Get them here as soon as possible."

"Right, sir."

"I'll have a look round here and come to your office when I'm through," Gideon said to Hellier.

"Very good, sir." The answer was almost mechanical. Hellier half-turned, and then added. "Thank you, sir. About the frog-man team."

"Fixed," Gideon said.

Singleton came off a telephone.

"They'll be on the way in five minutes," he declared.

While Gideon was looking over the Barnes sub-station of the Thames Division and Hellier was going through all the reports which had come in that day from the parks, the river banks, the neighbours and the school friends of the missing child, Geraldine herself was lying on her back and looking into the eyes of the man who sat rocking to and fro. The knife was no longer near him. He had given her some more milk and some biscuits. The scarf with which he had gagged her was in his hands, stretched taut. She managed to smile—a smile which seemed almost trouble-free.

"Please don't gag me again," she said. "I won't shout, I promise."

He gave her his slow, rather vacant smile.

He was thinking: "I couldn't use the knife, I couldn't stand the blood." Almost immediately he thought: "If I put this round her neck she couldn't talk and there wouldn't be any blood."

She wondered what was really passing through his mind, as she said again:

"*Please* don't gag me. I *promise* I won't shout."

But she would, of course, she would. He had no doubt. He would have to kill her and throw her body into the river, after dark. That was how he had disposed of her satchel, and it hadn't been traced to him. Her body wouldn't be, either.

At that precise moment the woman who had cycled away from the scene when the drag had caught something without knowing that it was a dog, turned into the street where the Pierces lived. She pulled up outside their house, rang the bell, and as Mrs. Edmond opened the door, she gasped:

"They've found the body! I saw them with my own eyes! They've found her!"

Wanda Pierce, in the kitchen of her neighbour's house, heard every word.

Chapter Seven

CONSPIRACY

Hellier, obviously determined not to overdo the deference, did not come out of his office to greet Gideon but simply stood up from his desk. It was a larger office than most, with a big pedestal desk looking disproportionately large because it was empty but for four trays, two with a few papers in them, and two telephones. Behind Hellier was a map of his district, on the right-hand wall a map of the Metropolitan Police Area, on the left a map of the Thames Division along its whole length.

Everything here was so clean it looked new; even the maps.

"Please sit down, Commander." Hellier's manner as well as his movements were stiff.

Gideon sat down. There was still nothing he liked about the man's manner, but he had learned from the Thames Divisional sub-station how completely Hellier was known to be on top of this job, and he was thoughtful about the signs of tension in the man which he had seen at the riverside.

"What makes you so sure the girl's in the river?" he asked.

"I'm not absolutely sure, sir. I would think it's a ten-to-one on chance."

"Any particular reasons?" asked Gideon.

"Her satchel was found in the mud on the bank. She was seen going towards the river. She was known to walk along the towpath, often alone, as it was only a slight detour on the way between her home and school. I've just had confirmation that her footprints have been found on a muddy patch, up to a place called the love nest." Hellier was too earnest to say this lightly. "That's a patch of shrubs frequently visited by courting couples."

"Any sign of her having been *in* the love nest?"

"No sir. But it's on a rise in the ground and it's bone hard there. We wouldn't see prints."

"Combed it?"

"Inside out. Would you care to see what I have done, sir?"

"Yes."

Hellier rose from his seat and crossed to

the Divisional map. Beneath it was a narrow shelf from which he picked up narrow strips of metal in many colours. He placed one after another on to the map and each stayed put; obviously they were magnetised.

"I've four groups working, as you know, sir. The blue strips represent men covering the river area in conjunction with Thames Division." He placed the blue strips into position. "Red is for my men who have interrogated the neighbours . . . green is for the men who have been and are searching all the parks, including Richmond Park . . . yellow is for the men who are working on the schools. If you will watch closely, sir . . . The areas shaded in pencil have already been covered once . . . The dead infant was found here." He put a black cross above a green strip. "The girl was last seen here . . . " As he went on Gideon was more and more impressed by his complete grasp and his computer-like mind. "I have personally questioned seven men whom I believe to capable of waylaying and raping the girl."

"How did you get on to them?" asked Gideon.

"Three have records of interfering with minors, two are suspect—they're known to hang about near the river and in the parks when the girls' schools are playing there, two were seen by all four girls when they were playing tennis. One is the local tuck-barrow man, I've had him watched for some time. He does a lot of hand-holding and head-patting—several parents have complained. I don't know of anyone else who can be considered an obvious suspect. I've a fairly complete list of men living alone—there are several in caravans near the river and on waste land, and a great many living alone in one room. One can find this out by studying the electoral register, sir—when there's only one person of the same name at any address, I have them checked. Comes in useful when co-operating with the Welfare Officer. All these are being visited in turn, sir, and I should have the last one questioned by nightfall. I've a hundred men on this operation, thanks to help from the Yard."

Gideon thought: All this, although he's convinced the girl's in the river. He searched for a way of saying he was impressed without being patronising when he heard a shout from outside, footsteps, a stentorian bellow of:

"Come back!"

More footsteps thundered, from stairs to landing, as Hellier moved swiftly towards the door. As he reached it, it burst open and he had to dodge aside to avoid its full weight. A wild-eyed man rushed in, grabbed Hellier by the lapels and began to shake him furiously.

"Where is she? Why didn't you tell *me* first? Why, you swine—"

Hellier could have crushed this man of lean build and medium height, but he backed away under the onslaught, while the man went on shouting and a plain-clothes man, and another in uniform hovered unhappily in the doorway.

Suddenly, Hellier said sharply:

"We haven't found your daughter, Pierce. Stop this nonsense." The violence seemed to be cut off, and Hellier shrugged himself free. "Who told you we had?" he asked.

"Someone—" Pierce half choked on the words—"someone said you'd pulled her out of the river."

"Then they were mistaken."

Pierce backed away. Hellier waved briskly to the men in the doorway and they closed the door without a word. Gideon moved quickly, thinking that Pierce might collapse; the colour drained from his face and he swayed, his eyes feverishly bright.

"But—she said she was there. She said she *saw* her."

"We found something but not your daughter," Hellier said. "If there had been any other discovery I would have been told by radio telephone." He moved stiffly to his desk, opened a cupboard and took out a bottle of whisky and a glass. He poured out a finger and gave it to Pierce, who stared at it vaguely, then suddenly raised it to his lips and tossed it down.

"For you sir?" Hellier asked Gideon.

"No, thanks."

Pierce muttered: "I thought my wife would kill herself. I really did. I—I rushed from the office when—when I heard. Mrs. Edmond telephoned me, she said—she said the other woman had *seen* Geraldine's body. Why did she lie?" His voice rose. "*Why did she lie?*"

Gideon laid a reassuring hand on his shoulder. "It was a mistake, Mr. Pierce.

Something was caught in the grab, and a lot of people thought it was your daughter. I'm very glad it wasn't."

"Isn't there—isn't there *any* news?" Pierce was suddenly terribly pathetic.

"No," Hellier said. "None at all."

"Not yet," Gideon tried to soften the blow. "I'm from Scotland Yard, Mr. Pierce, and in a life-time of experience I have never known a search for a missing person handled so swiftly or so thoroughly. The river is being searched as a precaution; every other possibility is being explored, including the possibility that your daughter has been abducted." After a brief pause to allow Pierce to speak if he chose to, Gideon went on: "All the Metropolitan Police and all the police of neighbouring counties are co-operating. I assure you truly that *everything* is being done."

Pierce muttered: "Oh, Oh, I see. Thank—thank you." He closed his eyes and pressed the tips of his fingers against his forehead. "Could you—could you say that to my wife? She doesn't—"

Hellier said awkwardly: "Commander Gideon has to go back to Scotland Yard."

Gideon said quickly: "I can go via Mr.

Pierce's house, if you think it will help."

"Oh, if only you will!" Pierce looked pathetically grateful. "My wife seems—seems to think that no one cares. Could you—" he hesitated, gulped, and went on hurriedly: "Could you drop me at my office? I really ought—ought to get back."

Startled, Gideon said "Must you go back to the office at a time like this?"

"It's—it's stocktaking time," said Pierce, miserably, "and Mr. Lee has cut up rough already. I'm the chief clerk, you see."

Gideon began: "Does he know—" and then he broke off. Obviously Pierce's employer must know, and there was no point in exacerbating the situation.

Hellier rang down for a car, and ten minutes later Gideon dropped Pierce off at a small block of offices near the Green, and was then driven round to Mrs. Pierce. It was a strange case for him to become involved in, but when he saw the woman he was glad that he had taken the trouble. She still had neighbours with her, and was nearly prostrate when he arrived; but the knowledge that it had been a false alarm, that her daughter might still be alive, put a thin flicker of fresh hope back into her.

Gideon was driven back through the summer beauty of Richmond Park, the trees heavy with leaf, here and there the scent of new mown grass. Soon he was back on the river, being taken slowly past the meadows, seeing the sweeping arches of the bridge, feeling an acute sense of nostalgia as he was reminded of the days of his youth when he had courted Kate along these very banks.

It was so peaceful and quiet . . . as if fear and violence belonged to a different world.

Fear and violence made up the world of Thomas Argyle-Morris.

When Carter and Cottingham had been remanded in custody he had felt at least that he had a breathing space. Now, he did not.

He was followed everywhere he went.

He knew the men; he knew their viciousness; he knew there was no cruelty of which they were not capable. He did not really know why they were after him, unless it was that they were friends of Carter.

Carter was bad enough; there was no doubt that Carter would gladly have drowned him and Mary Rose. He was vicious in his jealousy; when a girl was "his" she was his absolutely until he had finished with her. To this day, Argyle-Morris could not understand what had persuaded him to kiss Mary Rose; but that was over and done with. Dave Carter was the leader of the Cockles, and the Cockles were a small-time gang in the protection racket.

The men who were following Argyle-Morris belonged to a bigger and more powerful gang—a deadly gang. He knew of their existence, knew that Dave Carter sometimes worked for them, but he could not understand why they were so interested in Dave's love life.

Even in his fear, Argyle-Morris knew that this did not make sense.

But Screw Smith made sense.

Screw was a nickname which had grown up with Smith since, at the age of nine, he had seen a thumbscrew in a museum and had started to practise with a clamp on smaller or weaker children. By the time he was eleven, he had won his nickname.

Now, Smith could make anyone talk, simply by showing them the thumbscrew he had himself manufactured out of odd pieces of metal.

Why was he after him, Tom Argyle-Morris? *He* didn't know anything.

Argyle-Morris was sweating.

He was a shipping clerk who lived in one of the new blocks of council flats near Wapping High Street, with his mother and three sisters. He had a room of his own and he paid his mother three pounds a week for food and board, whether in a job or out—he preferred temporary posts, and made as much money as he needed by judicious smuggling and the selling of contraband. He spent very little time with the family. Now, in dread, he turned a corner and looked up at the flats. Each had a small balcony. Washing was blowing from some of them, while two women were talking on another. Above his own window, hanging geraniums trailed their vivid scarlet against the yellow brick wall.

He glanced round.

Screw Smith was fifty yards away, a little, carroty-haired man with very thin features and a pointed nose; a man whose cruelty showed in the twist of thin lips and the glitter in small, green eyes. Behind him was big, heavy Captain Kenway of the Salvation Army, the man in charge of the Army Canteen and refuge, who made a habit of going to see men whom the hostel had once housed; he was a one-man Auxiliary Probationer Service. He strode past Smith and glanced down.

Smith pretended not to notice him.

Argyle-Morris crossed the road hearing Captain Kenway's footsteps close behind him, feeling a kind of security in the shadow of the big man, who drew level on the far pavement.

"Hallo, Tom," he said. "Everything all right with you?"

"Sure. Sure, everything's fine." Argyle-Morris wiped the sweat off his forehead.

"Is your father back yet?"

"No, he won't be back much before October."

"That will be five months at sea—that's a long trip."

"He likes long trips."

"I know, I know," said Kenway. He was flabby and pale-faced and his lips as well as his hands were a little moist, but the expression in his eyes was very shrewd. "What's worrying you, Tom?"

"Nothing's worrying me!"

"If Dave Carter's boys are after you—"

"They're not after me, no one's after me!" If Smith saw him talking to the Army man it would get round that he was asking the Army for help, and they would skin him for that. He quickened his pace and almost ran into the big building. A lift was standing open. He pressed the fourth-floor button as a girl from a flat beneath his came running. The lift door nearly trapped her. Belatedly, Argyle-Morris held it back.

"Okay?"

She looked at him thoughtfully as the lift stopped at the third floor. He wiped the sweat off his forehead again and gulped as it went up to his floor. The door opened. The front door of his flat, nearly opposite, was closed. He opened it with a key and slipped inside.

He heard a quick movement—and Mary Rose appeared by the living-room door.

"You've got to save me," she gasped. "You've got to!"

"What—what the hell do you mean?" he muttered. "What's up?"

"They're after me." She could hardly get the words out.

"Don't be crazy, they're in clink."

"Not—not *them*, I don't mean *them*."

"Then who the hell *do* you mean?"

"Screw's lot!" she gasped. "Screw Smith's!"

Argyle-Morris clenched his teeth to try to stop them from chattering.

"You've got to tell them I don't know anything!" she went on fearfully. "You've got to make them believe you."

Feeling physically sick, he said. "You're crazy! No one's after you."

"You're lying to me. Screw's after you too, I *saw* him. He's down in the street now. You've got to tell him that I don't know anything." She grabbed his arm and half-dragged him into the living-room which was dominated by a huge television set in one corner. "Look down there!" she cried. "Is he there or isn't he?"

Tom Argyle-Morris peered down from the window. Screw Smith was crossing the road and looking up, as if he knew they were staring down. Mary Rose clutched Tom's arm tightly, and was gasping for breath, while he could hardly breathe, he was so frightened.

Smith reached the near pavement and then disappeared, beneath them.

"He's coming here," Mary Rose gasped. "I've got to get away—I've got to!"

A man from the doorway said very softly:

"Not until we want you to, doll."

Chapter Eight

THE WAREHOUSE

Mary Rose and Tom swung round.

A stranger to both of them moved forward, tossing a key into the air and letting it fall; it struck the floor sharply, brassily.

"I won't need that again," he said.

Mary Rose's fingers bit so deeply into Tom's arm that they seemed to burn. Her body was tight against his, too, as if she wanted to sink into him and so hide herself from this man with the sneering voice.

Tom muttered: "Where—where'd you get that key?"

"From your kid sister," the man answered. "I took it out of her handbag in the Supermarket—she's out shopping with her ma." The sneer was even more pronounced.

"Don't, don't let him hurt me," Mary Rose pleaded. "Don't let him hurt me."

"No one's going to hurt you," the man said, "unless it's Screw Smith."

She gave an agonised squeal.

"No, no, no, *no*!"

"Nice fingers and thumbs you've got, doll. Remember that." He glanced round and went on: "Okay, Screw, they're ready for you, all nice and ripe."

Screw Smith came into the room.

At close quarters he was vicious and cruel-looking; it was hard to believe that anyone could like him. He needed a shave and he needed a haircut, and when he raised his hands they showed up grimy, with blackened, broken fingernails.

"You talked to them?" he asked.

"I just told them the facts of life."

Tom moistened his lips and muttered: "I don't know what you want, I don't know anything."

"I don't, either. I swear I don't!" cried Mary Rose.

"Tom, you're coming along with us," Smith said. "We want a little talk."

"But I don't—"

"Shut up," Smith ordered. "You're coming."

"I'll call the cops! I'm not coming with you—I'll call the cops!"

As he spoke, both men moved with

bewildering speed, the stranger gripping Mary Rose's arm and wrenching it free, Smith kicking Tom savagely in the groin. Tom doubled over, clutching his stomach, and staggered about the little room. The stranger pulled Mary Rose to the table, dumped her into a chair, and forced her to lean back. Screw moved to her side and took her right arm, bare to the elbow. He stretched it across the table, hand palm downwards, and with his free hand took out the little instrument for which he was so notorious.

Mary Rose began to sob.

"I didn't know what I was doing, Screw, I swear I didn't. I got scared when he started kissing me, I thought you'd think it was my fault. But it wasn't, I swear it wasn't."

Slowly, Tom Argyle-Morris straightened up, his face grey with pain and terror. Yet there was shock in his expression, as if he could hardly believe the girl would say such things—would try to blame him, alone.

Smith said: "Okay, Tom. You come with us quietly, or the girl gets a squeeze from this. She likes being squeezed. If she wasn't a lying bitch you wouldn't be in this situation—*would you* ?"

"Oh, God. No, no, no," moaned Mary Rose. "It wasn't my fault, *it wasn't my fault*."

"Here's one squeeze she doesn't seem to want," Smith said. He spoke in a flat, emotionless voice, as he took her soft, white thumb between his thumb and forefinger; and the other man held her arm firmly on the table. She had nice hands, well-kept, and with beautifully shaped nails. "Coming with us Tom, old man? If you do, okay, Mary Rose can go and get herself cuddled by some other poor mutt."

"Tom," moaned Mary Rose. "Don't let them hurt me. You know it was your fault, you know it was."

Tom Argyle-Morris stared at her, gulped, then looked at Smith and muttered: "How do I know you won't hurt her if I come?"

"We won't need to, because you're going to tell us all we want to know."

Tom moistened his lips again. He didn't really blame Mary Rose but he felt she had let him down. He still felt the physical nausea from the kick, and it was worsened by a nausea of fear of what they would do to him. But if he didn't go with them then they would get to work on her, and he couldn't stand by and see them hurt a woman.

He said thinly: "I don't know a thing, but—but I'll come."

The stranger loosened his grip on Mary Rose's arm. Smith released her hand. She sat there, pale-faced, her eyes rounded into saucers, her fear despoiling her prettiness.

"Don't hurt him," she said weakly. "He didn't mean any harm."

"Okay," Smith said. "Let's go."

As they got into a black Ford Anglia parked outside the block of flats, Captain Kenway noticed them, noticed Argyle-Morris's pallor, and wondered uneasily what was going on. A quarter of an hour later he passed the flats again and this time saw Mary Rose come out, freshly made-up, her walk jaunty, her hips swaying provocatively. Captain Kenway stopped her.

"Mary Rose, is everything all right with Tom?"

She looked pertly into his flabby face.

"'Course it is, why shouldn't it be?"

she answered. "Excuse *me*, I haven't got time to stand here talking to *you*."

Tom Argyle-Morris sat in the back of the Ford Anglia, with Screw Smith; the other man drove along Wapping High Street, past the huge high warehouses with their drab-painted doors, past the Headquarters of the Thames Division Police, tyres grumbling over the cobbles. Soon they were going faster in a more open area; here more people were about, nice-looking girls, some wheeling prams, older women, a few old men with nothing to do, truck drivers, groups of men from the docks, capped and mufflered. Huge lorries lumbered past and towered over them, exhaust fumes, acrid, stifling, seeping into the car.

"Where are we going?" muttered Tom at last.

"You'll find out."

Ten minutes later they turned into the No. 2 Gate of the West India Docks. A Port of London Authority policeman stopped them, and Tom bit his lips and looked away.

"We're crew from the *Sugar Queen*," the stranger said.

"Got anything with you?"

"Nothing we didn't take out."

The policeman stared ruminatively, then waved a hand towards Tom.

"What's the matter with him?"

"He drank too much bad liquor, and he's paying for it," the driver said.

The policeman let them pass.

They drove along Poplar Docks, over the bumpy railway lines, past Blackwall Basin. Now and again through gaps in the big sheds they saw sugar freighters and banana boats, now and again they glimpsed the huge new buildings of the Granary and the Flour Company's mills. There was a lot of traffic, and no one took any notice of them. Cranes were being worked, and there was a constant clatter of noise from pneumatic drills used in the erection of new warehouses and new sheds. They slowed down near a small, green ship and Tom read the name: *Sugar Queen*.

Were they really going to take him on board?

The ship was being unloaded, two gangs were busy by the big open hatches, and the smell of fruit was strong, almost heady. Nearby were two big sheds, one with a hole gaping in the roof, another half-demolished by bulldozers and excavating machines. The noise was ear-shattering. The stranger swung the car into a side road between the two derelict buildings, then pulled in behind the one with the hole in the roof. On this side it seemed to be in fair condition.

"Out." Smith ordered.

Tom climbed out cautiously, still feeling shaky and slightly nauseated. Smith climbed after him, then caught hold of his arm and pushed him across the broken ground where weeds grew tall and grass was the only softness, into a doorway.

The driver revved his engine and drove off.

"Don't run," Smith ordered.

He kept his hand firmly on Tom's arm and led him across the big shed, which stank with rotting fruit which had been tossed there when sacks or crates were accidentally broken. It was nearly dark. Over in one corner was a huge pile of disused hogsheads, once used for bulk sugar, now replaced by metal containers. A gap had been cleared in this pile and Smith gave Tom a shove towards it.

"Keep going," he ordered.

There was hardly any light; only gloom and the stench and the noise. *Noise.* Tom kept shivering. *Noise.* Wherever Screw Smith worked there had to be noise to drown the sound of screaming.

Tom was sweating.

Then he stepped into an office, hidden by the hogsheads, clean and tidy, the walls lined with hardboard which kept some of the noise out. There was less stench in here, too, what there was being partially masked by the aroma of cigar smoke. High in an outer wall a closed window let in some of the light from outside. Lower down on the same wall were two strip lights, beneath which sat another man whom Tom Argyle-Morris had never seen before.

"We got him," Screw Smith announced with proud satisfaction.

The other man, big and massive, took a cigar out of his mouth, and spoke with a hard, guttural voice.

"Now all you've got to do is make him talk."

Tom gasped: "I don't know anything, I swear I don't!"

The big man said flatly: "You stole a

packet of industrial diamonds which was floating on the river near Fiddler's Steps, the night you and your girl ran away from Dave Carter. I want to know what you did with it."

Tom almost screamed: "It's a lie! I didn't know there was anything there! I don't know anything about any diamonds. You've got to believe me!"

The driver of the Anglia came in, walked straight to Tom, put a lock on his arm, then held the arm out towards Screw Smith.

In the exercise yard at Brixton Jail, Dave Carter said to Cottingham:

"They've just about started on Tom-Tom, now."

"You fixed him all right," congratulated Cottingham. "If they think he pinched those sparklers—"

"*Think*? They know, I made sure of that," Carter said, grinning. "Better they think *he* did, than me. If they hadn't gone down Fiddler's Steps I wouldn't even have known there was a racket going on."

"But you do now," Cottingham said. "I'll bet you turn the screw on when you get out of here."

"Don't make any mistake, I will," Carter asserted.

A warder drew near, disapprovingly, and they stopped talking.

Sydney Roswell was the Chief Superintendent of the North-East Division of the Metropolitan Police, the Division which covered the land area coinciding with that section of the Thames patrolled by the crews based on Headquarters in Wapping High Street. He was an elderly man, with a deep and exhaustive knowledge of his district, of the people in it, of the crimes which were carried on within its boundaries. He was also a deeply religious man who, when off duty, served a Methodist Church and the clubs associated with it, and also worked with other Christian groups in this rough and often brutal part of London.

The telephone on his desk rang, about the time that Tom Argyle-Morris was pushed into the secret "office" at Millwall Docks.

"Hello?"

"Captain Kenway of the Salvation Army is on the line, sir."

"I'll speak to him," said Roswell at once. "Hallo, Percy, I promised to ring you about that inter-denominational meeting, but—"

"I'm not calling about that," said Kenway. "I'm worried about a youth named Argyle-Morris, Thomas Argyle-Morris. Do you know him?"

Roswell sat up, startled.

"Yes. What about him?"

"I met him this afternoon and he was obviously badly worried. Frightened, I would say. And he was with Screw Smith. I'm sure you know who I mean, don't you?"

"I certainly do know whom you mean," agreed Roswell grimly. "Tell me just what happened, will you, Percy?"

As he spoke, Roswell opened a folder on his desk, marked: "*Diamond Smuggling—C. Supt. Micklewright*", and as the Salvation Army man recited what he knew, Roswell took notes in his own brand of shorthand.

Gideon had been back in his office for only ten minutes when his telephone rang. He felt pleasantly tired and relaxed, reassured by the thoroughness with which Hellier was working. It had been a smooth and wholly uneventful voyage back, with the sun behind his left shoulder most of the way and shining with striking effect on all the riverside buildings, old and new. He had stepped off by Westminster Bridge, as Big Ben struck five, and walked across to the Yard.

Now, picking up the receiver, he heard the operator say: "Sorry to keep you sir. Mr. Roswell of North-East is calling."

"I'll talk to him," Gideon said. He was almost glad to have something to take his mind off the memory of Pierce and his wife and the grief which they shared. "Hallo, Syd, what's on?"

"I would have talked to Micklewright but I can't get hold of him," Roswell said apologetically. "Remember Argyle-Morris, the youth who—"

"I remember," Gideon interrupted.

"Screw Smith seems to be having a session with him," announced Roswell.

Gideon said sharply: "Is he b'God! Do you know where?"

"Afraid not," said Roswell, as Gideon lifted the other telephone and dialled

Information. "He was driven off in a black Ford Anglia . . . " He told Gideon all that he knew.

Soon, Gideon was saying to *Information*: "Put out a call for Screw Smith and Thomas Argyle-Morris. I want to know where they are and where they've been. Send it to Thames Headquarters and the Port of London Police, ask Customs and the City Police to keep an eye open, too. And tell Mr. Micklewright I want a word with him." He rang off, made a few notes for Hobbs, then stood up and stared out at the river which was so much part of his life.

He could picture the beauty near Richmond.

He could picture the squalor in parts of the East End.

He could picture the curious way the water had risen, like a molten mound, over the corpse of a dog thought momentarily to be a child.

In a way, it was his river—all the romance, all the commerce and all the crime that its tides carried, were part of him. It held many secrets, secrets which it would seldom yield up to him as it did to such a man as Singleton. Old Man

River Singleton. Gideon smiled a little grimly. Singleton would be badly missed when he retired, but other men were slowly acquiring his knowledge of the river, men who already had a love for it. That was something Gideon had almost forgotten: the Thames Division men loved the river and were dedicated to keeping it as clear from crime as they possibly could.

This diamond smuggling might stretch them to the limit of their resources.

There was no way of telling himself why he suspected that, but suspect it he did. He hoped they would soon find Thomas Argyle-Morris. And the Pierce child. He wondered where Hobbs was, and when he would be back. And then, by some trick of memory, he remembered promising to let the insurance broker, Morris, have a detective on his staff, and he made a note.

Chapter Nine

FLOATING CASINO

"Alec, darling," Esmeralda Pilkington said. "I've a nasty feeling that you are going to be a policeman again. It isn't that I don't like policemen, but I can never get used to the fact that you're one. Jeremy hasn't done anything *very* criminal, has he?"

She was an attractive woman, in her middle thirties, with ash-blonde hair and a fair but slightly sun-bronzed face which made her eyes seem a very bright grey. Alec Hobbs had known her when she was in pig-tails and a gym tunic and he had been at Eton with her brother and Pilkington. She still had the figure of a girl, slim, thin-hipped, with shapely arms and legs. On this warm summer afternoon she looked fresh and elegant.

"He hasn't done anything criminal yet," said Hobbs, "he's just been his usual slap-happy self. Did you speak to him?"

"Yes, poor dear. He had to stay in

Paris for another night. Some difficulty, I understand, with the Paris models. He told me to give you every facility, Alec, and I've told Hugh St. John that *he* must, too."

"That's something," Hobbs said. "Where is St. John?"

"He's somewhere in London, I haven't any idea where, but he'll be back this evening. Why don't you come to dinner? You can talk it over then."

Hobbs was tempted.

There would be no harm in it, either; there was nothing in police regulations to say that he could not dine with an old friend and discuss business at the same time. But he came at last to the conclusion that with Esmeralda and Jeremy it would not be wise.

"I should love to," he said, almost too casually, "but I shall be working late."

Esmeralda stretched out and touched his hand.

"Still grieving, Alec?" When he didn't answer, she went on in a soft voice: "You shouldn't, you know. Helen would want you to be happy."

Had Gideon, had anyone else, said that

or anything like it, Hobbs would have stiffened with an aloofness not far removed from resentment. In a way, Esmeralda was very like a sister, and whatever motive she might have had in asking him to dinner, he knew she was now thinking, in genuine concern, only of him.

He smiled, quite freely.

"Yes, I grieve much of the time," he said. "But it isn't an obsession any longer, and it isn't why I work late so often. Believe it or not, the Yard is seriously under-staffed."

"I thought that only applied to policemen in uniform."

"They're worse off than we are, certainly," Hobbs agreed, "but there's a great deal of work waiting to be done, all the time. What I would like to do," he added before she could interrupt, "is go over the boat."

"*Now?*"

"Preferably now, yes."

"But Hugh isn't here—" she began, and then laughed and stood up; she moved with a deliberate slowness but was very graceful. "I suppose there's no reason why I shouldn't take you. That's if you don't mind me coming along."

"Esmeralda, dear," Hobbs said, "don't fish."

He got to his feet, and Esmeralda, slipping her arm through his, led him towards the garage.

Ten minutes later she was at the wheel of a grey Bentley, driving with nonchalant ease through the traffic in Park Lane, round the whirlpool of cars at Hyde Park Corner, then along Grosvenor Place towards Chelsea and the river. Hobbs glanced at her from time to time but she was never looking at him, was always on the alert for other cars, and obviously revelling in being at the wheel. Soon she was in Chelsea Bridge Road; she paused at the traffic lights, which turned from red to green almost at once, then turned on to the Embankment. It was very wide where she stopped, and comparatively quiet. She pulled in not far from the bridge, and they got out and walked towards the step which led down to the landing stages and pier.

This was a new one, installed for pleasure cruises only, and moored alongside were two large river steamers, one the *River Belle*, the other christened the

Belle Casino. Only a few men were about on the *Belle Casino*, but a small army was working on the *River Belle*. A young man with long hair and very tight trousers came hurrying to the gangway and helped Esmeralda on board.

"I'd no idea you were coming tonight, darling."

"Superintendent Hobbs persuaded me to bring him," Esmeralda said. "Superintendent, Timothy Gentian is in charge of all the arrangements for the actual show."

Hobbs had heard of but never met Gentian, who looked in his early twenties but must, thought Hobbs, be in his middle thirties at least. He had a high reputation as a dress designer, an equally high one as a choreographer. His eyes were clear, his skin fresh, there was something youthful and frank and zestful about him.

"How do you do, Superintendent." Gentian turned back to Esmeralda. "We had a Chief Inspector from the Thames Division here this afternoon to see what we were up to—he went off with Hugh to the Port of London Authority. I had no idea that one had to make plans in advance for a little trip up the river." He was only half-jesting. "Do come and see. . ."

Hobbs had seen the *River Belle* on a Saturday night, packed to the rails with roistering merrymakers, decks, salons, restaurants so crowded it was difficult to get through. He was astonished at the change. Gentian had draped the interior with velvet in pale greys and blues. Along the main deck were raised platforms, some of them already completed. Electricians and engineers were erecting flood-lighting, in a row of three lights were suddenly switched on, bright in spite of the sunlight. Hammering and banging was ceaseless—and so was Gentian's commentary.

"We're using the main *salon* for the girls and the two smaller bars for the male models, all the changing will be down there. The spotlight on the funnel—d'you see? —will be focussed on the main staircase, and the models will parade right round the ship . . .The seating is being made ashore, it shouldn't take long to erect . . . The buffet will be on one of the attendant boats which will be secured on the right hand side—do hope you're not a sailor, Superintendent!—and there will be a flotilla of smaller ships with the press, models of furs and gowns which can't all be stored on board. Newspapermen and furs will be ferried to and fro as it were. It has been a very complex arrangement to make."

"I can imagine," Hobbs said drily. "What else is planned for your guests?"

"Don't you think enough is being done?" asked Gentian. "They will see the finest collection of furs and gowns ever displayed, a magnificent display of jewellery, many of the world's most beautiful women. There will be a buffet with food of quite exquisite delicacy, and the best of wines. *Can* they ask for more?"

Hobbs smiled. "Some will."

"Alec, what *is* on your mind?" demanded Esmeralda Pilkington.

"Gambling," Hobbs said.

"Oh, the casino." Gentian spread his hands delicately. "That is available on the other boat for those with money to lose."

"Isn't it an official part of the show?" asked Hobbs.

"Show?" Gentian echoed deprecatingly. "No, Superintendent, it is *not* part of the presentation. An arrangement has been made I believe for our guests to become temporary members of the *Belle Casino* and to get aboard, but that is no part of my business."

"It's Hugh's though," Esmeralda pointed out.

They went ashore, Gentian handing Esmeralda over the side, and inclining his head slightly as Hobbs said goodnight. Hobbs walked with Esmeralda to the Bentley.

"Where can I drop you, Alec?" she asked.

"Parliament Square will be a great help," Hobbs said as they settled in. "Esmeralda—ask Hugh to come and see me tomorrow, will you?"

"But surely you *will* come and dine—"

"No," Hobbs said decisively. "Thank you, but I really must work."

"Alec," Esmeralda said as she slowed down outside Westminster Abbey, "you're worried about something to do with the show. What is it?"

"The presentation," Hobbs reminded

her, with a faint smile. "I don't want Jeremy to get himself into trouble, and from now on this has to be official police business. Just a formality," he added, and patted the back of her hand. "Thanks for the lift."

He saw that she glanced round as she drove off, but made no sign that he noticed, and walked briskly to the Yard, wondering whether Gideon had gone home, Big Ben struck the quarter; that would be a quarter past six, thought Hobbs, he might just catch him before he left.

Gideon was clearing up his desk when Hobbs tapped and entered from the passage door.

"Now what's on your mind?" Gidoen demanded, on the instant.

"Is it as obvious as that?" Hobbs asked wryly. "I've just come from the *River Belle*."

"What did you find on board?" Gideon was taking a bottle of whisky and some glasses out of a cupboard in his desk.

"I found enough to worry me," Hobbs said. "There will be a quarter of a million pounds worth of furs, at least as much jewellery, and a fortune on the casino boat. And all of that adds up to an almost irresistable temptation to thieves with ambition and ingenuity. Don't you think so?"

Gideon poured two drinks, and pondered as they drank. Finally, he said: "A damned sight too great. We must have that parade or whatever they call it guarded as if they were showing the crown jewels. We'll have to talk to Worby—" he hesitated. "Tell you what, Alec. We'll have Worby, Prescott and Singleton here for a conference, and it might be a good idea to have someone from the City Police and the P.L.A. There's a lot to discuss. Officially we can call it for these high jinks, and then tackle all the other things at the same time. Ten o'clock, say, in the morning."

"I'll arrange it," promised Hobbs, and finished his whisky.

"Another spot?" asked Gideon.

"No thanks—but I needed that one," Hobbs said.

Soon afterwards, Gideon was on his way home. Kate would be waiting for him and directly he began to think about her he realised that her first question would be about the Pierce child. He flicked on his radio and asked *Information* if there was any news from Richmond.

"Not a word," *Information* told him.

"Let me know at home if any comes in," Gideon ordered.

It was very dark in the quarry cave.

Geraldine lay still, very drowsy but aware that she was still alive. Now and again the man moved, but he offered no threat now; he was asleep. Gradually, full wakefulness came to the girl, and with it memory and fear—and hope.

She kept thinking about her captor.

She kept thinking about the way he fondled her, how he loved touching her skin.

She kept thinking about all that had happened since she had met him and allowed him to bring her here. She had known it was wrong, known it was risky.

She could almost hear her mother, too, warning her against men; there were times when she thought that her mother actually *hated* them.

"They only want one thing, and don't you forget it. Do you hear me, Geraldine?

They only want one thing, and when they've had it then they've finished with you. You're a big girl now, I've seen how attractive you are to men. Listen to me, darling . . ."

Now Geraldine was listening, over the months that had passed.

She was wide awake, and thinking, and remembering that strange look in the man's eyes, a kind of glazed expression, when he had held her scarf in his hands. She had been almost sure what was passing through his mind. He had gagged her again, not too tightly, and tied her to the bed before rocking to and fro, to and fro, until at last the rocking chair had stopped creaking.

He stirred.

Soon she realised that he was awake, too; she could just make out the shine of his eyes. The chair creaked again and she knew that he was getting up. He came across to her and she felt his hand groping about her, about her shoulders, then about her face. He fumbled with the scarf behind her head, loosened it, then drew it away. Without a word, he moved to one side; a match flared, dazzling her. When she opened her eyes wide again she saw a candle, flickering slightly. The light grew stronger, but when he came to her again his body hid the actual flame. Gently he began to massage her cheeks and chin and mouth. Soon, he loosened the rope round her waist, helped her to sit up, and held a cup to her lips.

It contained milk, cold and greasy and none too fresh, but it eased the dryness in her mouth, her parched throat, and she drank eagerly.

When she had finished she drew her head back. "You're nice," she told him. To her, the words sounded hoarse and over loud. Be natural, be natural, she told herself.

"What did you say, child?" he asked.

"I said you were nice," Geraldine repeated. "Very nice."

He looked at her eagerly. "Do you really think so?"

"Of course I do. I think you're very nice, and—I love you touching me."

"You—you *do*?" His voice grew shrill.

"Yes," she whispered. "I really do."

She felt his hands upon the satin smoothness of her legs.

She heard him draw in his breath, as if he had difficulty in breathing. He pressed harder. She wondered what he was thinking, believed that while he was doing this at least he would not kill her.

He was thinking with a kind of exalted desperation: She likes me . . . If she likes me she won't shout . . . *If* she likes me. Perhaps it's a trick. Perhaps she's lying to me. If she's lying to me I'll choke the life out of her, I'll choke her to death.

She whispered again: "You're very nice."

She was not yet fourteen.

Chapter Ten

CONFERENCE

Gideon opened the door of his office at half-past eight next morning, and found Hobbs sitting at his desk, telephone in hand. He waved to Hobbs to stay where he was and glanced through a file of reports on a corner of the desk.

Hobbs said into the telephone: "Then you'll have to put it off. Be here at ten—Commander Gideon's office." He rang off and stood up. Whereas Lemaitre would have grumbled about whoever was raising difficulties and named them, Hobbs made no reference to what had just occurred, saying only: "That's everyone."

"Nice and early," Gideon said drily. He felt in a brisk, assertive mood this morning, without knowing why. The day was dull outside and the atmosphere sticky and unpleasant. "Anything new about the Pierce girl?"

"No."

"The baby killing?"

"Hellier is questioning a girl now—he seems pretty sure she's the right one."

"Micklewright?"

"Nothing new—except that he seems to be getting on all right with Van Hoorn."

"We'll see them at lunch." Gideon said.

"I wondered if it would be a good idea to have Micklewright in on the conference," Hobbs said.

Gideon frowned. "Why?"

"He's been concentrating on the river, and he may have something useful to contribute," answered Hobbs.

Gideon's frown deepened.

"I suppose so. And you're right in principle anyhow—I should have thought about it. We want to talk to the City and the P.L.A. people about both the parade and the smuggling, and ought to have the Customs here, too." He was annoyed with himself because he hadn't thought of these things before. "Kill two birds with one stone," he added, feeling once again that he was speaking tritely.

"I asked the P.L.A. to check if Customs could have men available if we should need them," Hobbs told him.

Gideon's frown faded into a wry, amused grin.

"That's good—we will have 'em all." He looked round the office. "Can't get 'em all in here, though. Better use the small conference room. Have coffee laid on for eleven-fifteen."

"I'll do that," Hobbs promised.

"Is there anything new?" asked Gideon.

"Nothing which need worry us this morning," Hobbs assured him. "There was a small bank raid at Lewisham yesterday afternoon and a post office was broken into during the night at Chelsea."

"Any news of that chap with the high-falutin' name? Argyle-Morris?"

"No."

"I'll talk to Roswell," Gideon said. "You carry on."

Hobbs nodded, picked up some of the papers, and went out. Gideon leaned back in his chair, drumming his fingers on his desk. He suspected that there was something on Hobbs' mind which he didn't yet want to talk about. Oh well, he'd just have to wait until Hobbs decided to mention it. Stretching for the telephone, he put in a call to Roswell.

It came through almost at once.

"No, nothing's turned up," Roswell said. "Not even Argyle-Morris."

"What does that mean exactly?" Gideon asked.

"He didn't come home last night."

"What about the girl?"

"She's home and as bold as brass," replied Roswell. "You'd think they'd learn, wouldn't you?"

"Learn what?"

"She nearly gets drowned because she plays fast and loose with Dave Carter, and now that the new boy friend's away for a night she's up most of it with another one. We kept an eye on her after Argyle-Morris left with Screw Smith."

"Who's her third boy friend?" asked Gideon, thoughtfully.

"Not one of Carter's gang, as far as we can find out," Roswell said.

"Might be a good idea to check very closely on him," said Gideon.

"If you think so, George."

Gideon only just bit back a rough: "I do think so." Roswell was old in the service and a little inclined to take things easily. He was equally inclined to feel that only he really knew how to handle his Division; and in one way he was right. Gideon rang off and pushed thought of the Divisional man from his mind—and almost at once the telephone rang.

"Mr. Hellier of Richmond for you, sir."

Gideon's heart began to beat faster.

"Put him through . . ." there was a short pause. "Good morning, Hellier."

"Good morning, sir." Hellier's voice betrayed no emotion at all. "We haven't found the body in the river, for what that's worth. The frogmen finished half an hour ago."

"So the child may still be alive." Gideon's voice was gruff.

"Could be, sir." There was a fractional pause before Hellier went on: "I've just talked to the young mother who killed her infant child."

"She admitted it, did she?"

"Yes, sir. She's seventeen. Parents haven't helped at all. I'm charging her this morning and asking for remand in custody. The Welfare people can see what they can do, then."

"Right." Gideon wondered whether this was all Hellier had called him about.

"One other thing, sir," Hellier went on. "There's a possibility that Geraldine Pierce is on the other side of the river." He meant, 'not in my division', and that told Gideon a great deal. Obviously he was not sure that the police on the other side would search in the way he thought necessary. "So far we've taken it for granted that she's on this side, sir."

Gideon could have said: "I haven't taken anything for granted." In fact he said: "I'll have a word with them."

"Thank you, sir."

"What was that about Pierce losing his job?" asked Gideon.

"His employer is an old skinflint," answered Hellier, "but I don't think he'll be fired, he's too useful. His boss may make life hell for him, but he won't cut off his nose to spite his face."

Gideon grunted and rang off.

"Pierce, you're nearly an hour late again this morning," Edward Lee said to his chief clerk. "You know how important this stock-taking is. I have no objection to you leaving early if you've finished, but you must be here on time."

Pierce thought: You humbug, you know you expect me to work overtime every night. He said: "It's a very worrying time, sir."

"I appreciate that. Nevertheless . . ."

As he listened, Pierce gritted his teeth and clenched his hands; and when at last he was alone at his desk in a tiny office, all he could see was first his wife's face, then Geraldine's, dancing before his eyes.

He turned to the stock cards.

In a way it was better to have something to do.

Gideon was five minutes late getting to the small conference room, delayed by a telephone call from Oslo about some forged öre notes being circulated in the United Kingdom. It was probably just as well, for Worby was only just arriving, and he prided himself on his punctuality.

The room was almost filled by an oval table of light-polished walnut, with ten chairs around it. In front of each man was a note pad and pencil, between each two an ashtray. The window was small and high, overlooking the main courtyard. It was open, and the noise of cars starting up, of men talking, of men laughing, drifted into the room. Each chair had wooden arms and the largest was one of three which were vacant. Gideon took it.

Hobbs was on his right; Worby, dark, well-preserved, a little too heavy at the jowl, was on his left. Micklewright sat next to Worby, big knuckly hands clasped on the table in front of him. Next to him was Chief Superintendent Prescott of A.B. Division; next to him in turn, Roswell of N.E. These two men might have been father and son, Roswell looking older than his fifty-nine years, balding, grey, with creases in his forehead and jowl, and unexpectedly merry blue eyes, while Prescott, of similar build, bore the same creased face, the same hint of enjoying life to the full. Next to Prescott was Superintendent Yates of the City of London Police, big, blond, military-looking, with a high complexion, improbably curly hair, and china blue eyes. He seldom said anything at conferences, only after them.

Gideon knew all of these men well.

He also knew Superindentent Hennessy

of the Port of London Authority Police, for before joining the Port of London Authority Force Hennessy had been in the Metropolitan Force, resigning at sergeant's rank because he could not get what he so badly wanted—transfer to the Thames Division. Hennessy was a spare time yachtsman who loved the water. He was short compared with the other men, stocky, with very broad shoulders, nearly black hair and well-marked eyebrows, a rather beetling forehead and a broad snub nose.

On either side of the Port of London Authority man were Customs officers—one of whom Gideon recognised as Nielsen, a senior officer in the Water Guard branch which dealt with crews, passengers and ships' stores. Nielsen was a fine-looking, fair-haired and fair-complexioned man, of mixed English and Swedish parentage. The other, obviously from the Landing Branch of the Customs service, had charge of cargoes both going out of and coming into the Port of London. He was the youngest-looking man present.

Hobbs turned to Gideon. "I think you know everyone except Mr. Cortini of the

Customs Landing Branch, Commander."

"How are you, Mr. Cortini?"

"Commander."

"Good of you all to come at such short notice," Gideon said, and saw Prescott shoot a smug glance at Hobbs; so probably he had been the one to make difficulties. "The major problem is this mannequin parade that's been sprung on us. As it's going as far as Greenwich it goes through all our divisions and spheres of influence."

"Sprung on us is right," said Worby. "We'll only just have time to make arrangements."

"What arrangements need take all that time?" Prescott asked.

"Don't need telling you're a landlubber," Worby retorted. "We've got to make sure the river's clear—no big vessels moving in and out, or they swamp the little boats. We've got to check the tide, make sure it's not likely to be high, and patrol the river for the idiots who'll hire boats and get as close as they can to all that mink. And once the pleasure boats get wind of the river parade they'll put on special trips or divert their regular trips up and down the river. Every water man with a small boat and a wife will be there—and most of their families, too."

Worby wiped the sweat off his forehead as he finished and even Prescott looked slightly abashed.

Gideon asked mildly: "Anything you can't cope with, out of all that?"

"Not if everything goes to plan," said Worby. "But one boat capsizing, or one model falling overboard, could make a lot of difference."

"Overtime laid on?"

"Yes—oh, we'll manage, Commander. I've got all the specials on duty, too."

"Haven't lost much time," Gideon approved. "What about the bridges?"

"Bound to be crowded," remarked Roswell.

"Crammed," agreed Banks.

"A general rider for double duty for all traffic police has gone out," Hobbs reported. "I've followed the general plans for the *Evening News* pageant. The same streets will be non-parking areas after two o'clock in the afternoon, and I've warned London Transport to be ready for extra demands for buses and trains."

"Do you really think it will be *that*

big?" demanded Roswell, sceptically.

"I think it might."

"Could be a damp squib," Prescott objected.

"Then we'll be able to send everyone home early," Gideon said soothingly. "Better that than be caught half-prepared."

"Can't understand why they haven't given us more warning," Worby complained. "Pilkington isn't a fool—didn't he have something to do with the Fire of London pageant?"

"He co-ordinated the plans for the business houses floats," said Hobbs stiffly.

"Thought there was something, Geor—Commander," Worby frowned. "Pilkington *must* have known what a sensation this would cause. Given a fine night we'll have a million people by the river. Londoners love to see any kind of pageant, and mannequins on parade will draw them like bees round a honey-pot."

Gideon thought: Yes. And it is puzzling. Aloud, he asked: "Does this affect you, Mr. Cortini?"

"We've been told there will be two ships from Calais with a bonded cargo of furs," Cortini said. "The jewellery from the Continent is coming in by air."

Gideon wrote *Airport P* on his note pad.

"This is rather an exceptional case, Commander," the Customs man went on. "As the furs won't be unloaded on land but simply transferred to the *River Belle*, they won't strictly be liable for duty, but the moment any of them are sold they become liable. And they may be sold on board the ship and brought ashore by the buyers—they sometimes prefer to do this rather than have them delivered."

Gideon frowned. "That's a point."

"Didn't think of that," said Hennessy.

"Even the P.L.A. forgets things sometimes," said Cortini drily.

"What are you going to do?" Gideon asked.

"The organising committee has put up a bond. The purchasers will be charged the usual import and purchase tax rates, and we'll get a copy of the bill to keep the record straight when the organisers clear the bond."

"There's a good chance that someone will cheat, surely," Hobbs remarked.

Cortini smiled drily. "I'll have men

mixing with the guests. So will Nielsen."

"I have ten men detailed," Nielsen boasted. "It isn't that I think anyone will deliberately cheat, but just in case they fall to temptation."

There was a general chuckle.

"How *did* we get to this?" asked Banks. "Until Hobbs phoned me, I hadn't an inkling."

"The insurance broker involved was worried," Gideon answered.

"Can't say I blame him," said Roswell, his scepticism dispersed. "The more I think about this the crazier I think it was to hush it up for so long. There's a limit to stunt advertising. If we're not careful we'll have a great River Robbery on our hands. There could be upwards of a million involved in this show."

"We're here to make sure that nothing goes wrong," Gideon said, mildly.

"No need to worry about them getting away with a River Robbery as they did with the Great Train job," Worby said reassuringly. "You land chaps forget that you can't move around on the river like you can on land. Big ship or little boat, it has to be secured, has to be unmoored, has to get under way slowly. You can't hurry when you start anything on water. That's why we have little real crime on the river. Why, there wasn't more than a hundred thousand pounds' worth stolen last year!"

"As far as you know," said Roswell slyly.

"We know how much is lost from stuff coming into the port," said Hennessy, "but a hell of a lot is almost certainly lost on ships going out. Don't discover the loss until it's at the port of destination, that's the trouble."

Two or three others made a comment and Gideon did not interrupt, for he was brooding over what Roswell had said. There *was* an obvious risk. And if any group of criminals knew of the parade in time, they might well plan a raid—and if they did, then they would make as sure as possible that they could get away with it.

Could they?

He felt uneasy, without quite knowing why, but at least he was satisfied that all normal precautions had now been taken. He must give Micklewright his head soon.

The man was obviously unable to restrain his impatience.

He was about to change the subject to the industrial diamonds case when the telephone rang.

"I gave instructions that we shouldn't be disturbed," Hobbs said, lifting the receiver. "Who . . ." He broke off almost at once, and handed the instrument to Worby. "It's your man Singleton, he says you told him to call you it he had any news of Argyle-Morris."

"So I did," Worby said. "Excuse me, Commander . . . Yes, Jack, what is it?" There was a pause before he went on in an ominous voice: "Oh, *has* he."

Chapter Eleven

RIVER'S VICTIM

All that Tom Argyle-Morris could think of was pain.

There was pain in his thumb, awful pain in his thumb; and in his face, his eyes, his mouth, his stomach, his chest. Everywhere.

He was so full of pain that he could hardly remember how it had begun, who was causing it. He was hardly aware when they were asking questions or shining blinding lights into his eyes.

He was on fire with pain.

No one had spoken for some time, he was aware of that; no one had shone the light, no one had touched him. Yet they seemed still to be there, menacing shapes and sounds hovering or whispering close by. He knew that he was quivering, that he could not keep still, that there was warmth on his hands and fingers, on his toes.

But no one seemed to be touching him now.

He felt himself lifted, suddenly, and tried to scream, but hardly a sound came from his lips. He was lifted. Oh God, what next, what next? He was carried. A man stumbled and brought fresh waves of agony. He felt coolness—he was out of doors. He felt himself pushed into the back of a car. Was it an ambulance? The doors closed behind him with a bang.

The car moved.

Every bump was agonising, every swerve at a corner, every railway line. They were taking him out of the docks.

To hospital—please God, to hospital.

Soon they drove over a smooth road and now only the vibration of the engine hurt. At last he opened his eyes—and found that it was dark. He could see street lamps and lighted windows, that was all. He closed his eyes again. Suddenly the car stopped, and he heard the men coming towards the back, rubber soles making little noise. The doors were opened. He tried to raise his head but a hand closed over his face and rammed him down with a thump which sent new waves of agony through his naked body. They pulled him out savagely, one holding him by the ankles, another by his wrists.

He felt them running.

He opened his eyes and saw light shining on the water.

Terror struck him dumb as they swung him to and fro three or four times and then let him go.

He had his mouth wide open in a vain attempt to scream when he struck the water. He tried to struggle but he could not stop himself from going down.

It was Superintendent Jack Singleton, out with his crew next morning, who saw the tell-tale mound of water which always rose above a floating body. It was Sergeant Tidy who used the hitcher and the drag to pull the body in. It was Singleton who took one look at the bruised and battered face, another at the pulped thumb, and who felt sick.

The senior officers gathered about the table at the Yard were silent, Worby listening, the others—including Gideon

—looking at him with tense interest. Finally Worby said:

"Yes, pull her in . . . And pick up that man she was with last night . . . and pick up all of Carter's gang for questioning . . . Every one of the sons of bitches, yes."

He rang off, then turned to Gideon. "Thomas Argyle-Morris was pulled out of the Thames half-an-hour ago. He'd been tortured—savaged—and tossed in. Singleton thinks he was thrown in near Fiddler's Steps—there's a current which carries flotsam from there to the place where the body was found."

The Customs men, who knew nothing of the significance of this, looked their curiosity. Micklewright cracked his knuckles, and said:

"Well, Carter didn't do *that*."

"It's not a Carter gang job," said Worby, with absolute assurance. "He'd beat a man up but he wouldn't torture him. We want Screw Smith and we want to know who Screw's been working for."

Hobbs said: "I'll go down to *Information*."

"Yes," said Gideon. He stopped himself from telling Hobbs what to do and waited until the door closed on the Deputy Commander. Then he looked at Micklewright.

"Will you tell us just what's happening about these industrial diamonds, Mick? And where this murder comes into it."

Micklewright straightened up, momentarily taken by surprise, then launched into the story with a lucidity that could not have been greater had he prepared a report for this very moment. Something of his awkwardness seemed to fall away from him, he became a police officer of obvious acumen. He told of the Dutch concern over the extent of the losses, of Van Hoorn's visit, of the evidence that the packet found by the Thames Division patrol was one of those stolen from Amsterdam. Then, taking the actual waterproof container from his brief-case, he went on:

"Amsterdam says that four or five lots, worth between two and three thousand pounds each, are stolen every month. And a lot of uncut diamonds are stolen, too. That makes it very big business. If Argyle-Morris was killed because he was involved and might have talked, then we know the organisation is big enough for the criminals to take murder in their stride."

Into the silence which followed, Roswell asked in a small voice: "Big enough to think up a Great River Robbery?"

Van Hoorn's guttural voice had a penetrating quality which could be heard all over the dining-room. Gideon, seldom self-conscious, was very aware of the attention the Dutchman was attracting during the hour he spent with him and Micklewright. And he could see the signs of rebellion on Mickelwright's face as Van Hoorn kept saying:

"It was as I said in the beginning, Commander, there is a big criminal organisation which buys stolen industrial diamonds here in England. Where else they go I do not know. It is easy for anyone to steal, yes, but as I said in the beginning, who would steal if they did not know there was a buyer?"

Micklewright said: "The Inspector thinks there is a widespread sales organisation in this country, Commander."

"What makes you think this, Mr. Van Hoorn?"

"I go to Oslo, Stockholm, Copenhagen, Brussels, Paris—all the cities of Europe. I am told by the diamond merchants that sales are lower everywhere—ten per cent, fifteen per cent. But the industrial users, what do they say? They say they *use* more. Commander, industrial diamonds, as you well know, are used in precision engineering and—"

Micklewright made a grimace, his lips appearing to form unspoken words, the last two of which seemed to be: ". . . suck eggs."

". . . So we have more diamonds used, less diamonds sold," Van Hoorn remarked. "And we have many diamonds stolen. It seems to me a matter of certainty, Commander—these stolen diamonds are placed on to the market by illegal sellers, at low prices."

"Can you prove that?" asked Gideon.

"Not yet, sir. It is a difficult matter to prove. Industrial users who buy unofficially do not wish the source of their supplies to be known."

Micklewright leaned forward in his

chair. "All right, then you think there is a big organisation which sells the diamonds. But why insist that its headquarters are in England? Why not *Holland*? Or if it comes to that, America? They're the world's super salesmen. And they have access to the South American diamond supplies. Why pick on us?"

Van Hoorn spoke almost angrily. "But I have told you. We have arrested one known thief, he comes to England often by air. And you yourselves find the diamonds in the river. It is easy to send them from Holland to England and easy for England to absorb them, she is so much a bigger country than Holland. Commander, I say to you—I believe in England there is the heart of a big diamond smuggling and stealing ring—very big indeed. I ask that you request Superintendent Micklewright not to shrug his shoulders at this."

"If it exists, we'll uncover it," Gideon said soothingly. "How long will you stay in London?"

"I have to return tonight for conferences, but the day after tomorrow I come back."

"Can you wait for five days before coming back?" asked Gideon.

"Five *days*?" The Dutchman looked startled. "May I ask why, Commander?"

"We shall be having one of the biggest searches of the river in the next five days," Gideon told him, "and an opportunity to examine the possibilities very closely." He turned to Micklewright. "Did you tell the Inspector about Argyle-Morris?"

Micklewright looked uneasy. "No." His hands, large, ungainly, moved clumsily, knocking against the handle of his knife; dripping with thick gravy, it fell on to his trousers. "Oh, what the hell," he muttered.

"I will, of course, wait five days," Van Hoorn said. "And Commander, permit me to say how kind you are to spare this luncheon for me. I am deeply honoured."

"Pleasure," Gideon made himself say, and was glad it was over.

"Mick," Gideon said, in his office after the luncheon. "What's worrying you?"

"That damned Dutchman," Micklewright muttered.

"I thought you were getting along with him nicely."

"That was before he manufactured a big anti-Dutch plot by some master minds among English criminals. It's just as easy to smuggle stuff into Germany and France from Holland."

"But he's found no evidence of that whereas he has found evidence that some are coming here," said Gideon. "You're not giving him a fair crack of the whip, Mick. He could be right. In any case we've got to make sure whether he is or not." Slowly, he went on: "When did you last have a holiday?"

"In the spring. But I'm not over-tired, if that's what you mean." Micklewright bridled.

"Then what *is* the trouble?"

"Forget it, George." Micklewright spoke harshly. "I'm getting old and I don't like Continentals. That's about the size of it."

Even more deliberately Gideon went on: "Would you like to be relieved of the job?"

Micklewright went very still; and for a long time the office was silent. Then he pushed his chair back, and said stiffly:

"That's up to you, Commander."

"If I relieve you of the job, what will Clara say?" Gideon demanded.

"*Clara*? *She* won't care." Micklewright sounded bitter, but the next moment he recovered himself. "Nothing to do with Clara, anyway," he added hurriedly. "Is that all, Commander?"

So it's trouble at home, thought Gideon. He saw the misery on the other's face, and for a few moment's could think of nothing to say. Certainly it wouldn't help to pursue the Clara issue now, this would only drive Micklewright further back into his shell. "Well, Van Hoorn's off your back for a few days," he said at last. "Keep at it yourself, and if you need help, let me know. It's beginning to look as if Argyle-Morris was killed by some pretty nasty customers, and it could be tied in with those diamonds. We don't know that he wasn't trying to escape with them, do we?"

"He swears—he *swore* when we talked to him, that he'd never seen the packet. Don't think I'd overlook a simple possibility like that, do you? I'll ask Worby to find me a desk down at Wapping for the next few days. That all right?"

"Yes," said Gideon.

Micklewright stood up, moved towards

the door, hesitated, then said awkwardly:

"Thanks, George."

He went out.

"Warbler," Gideon said to Chief Superintendent Worby, "Micklewright's going to work from your manor for a few days. Keep an eye on him, will you?"

"Still on the bottle, is he?" Worby asked.

"Something's eating him," said Gideon slowly. "And I'd like to know what." He rang off and sat back in his chair, wondering whether he should have gone so far. Worby and Micklewright were old friends and Worby would know that he, Gideon, was genuinely concerned for the other man, but it wasn't good to have one senior officer watching another.

The truth was that if Micklewright went on as he was going he could no longer be trusted with major assignments. It did not matter how sorry one was for a man, the police had to get results—and results only came from detectives who could give their very best to the job.

Making a conscious effort, he put Micklewright out of his mind, turning his thoughts towards Sir Jeremy Pilkington's parade. A show of jewellery and an international ring of diamond thieves. It had to be a coincidence. Gideon kept turning it over in his mind, then went over what had been said and planned at the morning conference; at least they'd had *some* warning.

Supposing a ring of jewel thieves *did* use the river for hiding and delivering precious stones . . . and supposing the same ring decided to try to stage a robbery at the parade . . . couldn't the hiding places and the disposal plans for the industrial diamonds be used for the more valuable jewellery?

Fanciful? he wondered.

He'd known stranger things happen.

It was nearly seven o'clock when he left his office and drove back to his home in Fulham. As he opened the front door, he heard Kate coming along the passage; so she had seen him and, he guessed, was excited about something.

Almost at once, she said: "George, you didn't tell me about the River Parade."

"What do you know about it?" Gideon asked in surprise.

"Four invitations were delivered by hand only twenty minutes ago," Kate told him, "*and* a brochure! It looks as if it's going to be magnificent."

It was good to see her so pleased, and Gideon made a mental note to tell Hobbs about her pleasure. It was less good to see her expression, at the dining-table, as her thoughts obviously veered to something unpleasant.

"George," she said. "Do you think there's any hope for that Pierce child?"

Chapter Twelve

TO KILL OR NOT TO KILL

"What's your name?" asked Geraldine Pierce timidly.

The man said roughly: "Never mind my name!" He rolled off the bed and stood glaring down at her, his face demoniac in the candlelight. "What do you want to know my name for? Go on, tell me!" He thrust his hands on to her shoulders and shook her violently, banging her head up and down on the hard pillow. His voice rose. "*What do you want to know my name for?*"

In her terror the child gasped: "Don't shout! People will hear you. Don't shout!"

The warning stopped him; people did come down to the quarry, especially children. He drew back, releasing her, and his rasping breath seemed to go in and out in time with her shallow, frightened breathing. It was very quiet. The candle flickered in a faint breeze from the door. After a while he leaned over her again but this time he did not touch her.

"Go on, tell me, why do you want to know my name?"

"I—I want to call you something, that's all."

"You don't have to call me anything."

"I—I just wanted to."

"Why did you want to?"

She was still taking in those quick, shallow breaths as she stared up into his face.

"I—I *like* you," she said. And after a pause, she added: "*You* know *my* name."

"Yes, I do. *Geraldine*. But that doesn't mean you have to know mine. You can like me without knowing my name." He nodded, as if to emphasise the fact that his argument was unassailable.

Geraldine hesitated before beginning:

"I know, but—"

"But what?"

"It doesn't matter," she said wearily.

"It matters to me!"

"I'm sorry," she said. "I just wanted to know. I thought it would be friendlier."

"You're not lying to me, are you?"

"Of course I'm not! Why on earth should I?"

"You could want to know my name so as to tell somebody."

"Who—who is there to tell?" she asked helplessly.

He frowned, then lowered himself to the rocking chair and drew it closer to the bed. She watched him uneasily. He was like one of the younger kids at school, it didn't matter what she said he would find an objection, no matter how silly. He *did* behave like a child; like her father did, sometimes, when her mother had vexed him. This time he did not answer but placed his hand gently on her leg, just above the knee. He *was* gentle when he was stroking her, whenever their bodies were close; touching. Except when he was angry about some imagined slight or genuine fear, he was very gentle.

"You can call me Dick," he said.

"Oh, that's lovely!" She was about to ask if that meant that his name was Richard, but thought better of it. "Dick—that's a *very* nice name."

"Do you really like it?"

"Yes, I do. It's *lovely*."

"I'm glad you like it," he moved his hand gently upwards.

"Do you like that?"

She felt the pressure of his hand. She felt the stirring of a strange excitement which she had already felt with him—and sometimes when she had thought about "men", when on her own.

"Do you?"

She whispered: "Yes. Yes, Dick, I do."

"Do you—mind—what I do?"

"No," she said. "No. I—I love it."

And in a way, she did.

And in another way, she knew that she must humour him. Because when they were close together she was not tied and helpless.

And—once—he had nearly dropped asleep.

If he was asleep and she was free she could creep off the bed and get out of this awful place.

Afterwards . . .

Afterwards, exhausted, he lay by her side, breathing very heavily. Soon Geraldine began to think that he *was* asleep He was on the outside of the bed but she could slide downwards and climb off the foot. That was the only way. She began to ease herself downwards and he did not stir.

She felt her legs go over the foot of the bed. Scarcely breathing, she managed to touch the floor. Then she was on her knees at the foot of the bed. The candle-light shone on the back of his head and his bare shoulders. Slowly, cautiously, she stood up, and turned towards the door. She did not know that this door had been built, in the first place, to keep out draughts; that outside it was concealed by rocks and sand, with only just room to squeeze through.

She reached the door, glancing fearfully back at the huddled figure on the bed. She saw her own shadow, dark and gigantic against the cave wall; almost frightening her. Then, feeling for the handle, she turned it, slowly, gently, and pulled.

The door did not move. She pulled again, but still it did not move. Looking up, she saw that it was bolted. Standing on tiptoe she began to slide the bolt back, but this wasn't easy. Holding her breath she went on, exerting more and more pressure—until suddenly it shot back, and metal struck metal with a noise like a bullet shot.

She heard Dick move.

She snatched at the handle but the door still did not open. Terror rose up in her as she heard the bed creak. He sprang from it and swore at her just above his breath, vicious, filthy words. She swung round before he reached her, to try to fend him off, and felt his fingers tough her neck and then slide off.

"No!" she gasped. "No!"

He seized her by the neck and she felt his thumbs pressing into her windpipe and she knew that she was near to death. She slumped against him, pleading with her body, making no attempt to struggle, sensing that it would be useless to try.

As she leaned her weight against him, he had to bend his arms at a more difficult angle and there was less strength in his grip. Now she could breathe more freely. She sobbed as if her heart was broken, put her arms round him and pressed against him, looking up into his face, her lips parted in an invitation which was unthinking and wholly natural.

Gradually his anger began to die away.

Gradually, his grip on her neck slackened.

"Don't ever do that again," he said. "Don't ever do that again."

She felt the change in him as his hands

fell gently to her shoulders and he began to caress her. The tumult in her heart quietened and soon she began to doze.

She was going to tell the police, Jonathan Jones thought.

She would have told them all about me.

She's very lovely, but she won't be any use to me if they take me away.

So long as I can keep her here, he thought, everything will be all right.

The following morning Hellier stood in his big office, studying the progress of the magnetised markers and the reports which had come in from all the groups of officers. There was no sign at all of the missing child.

If she's dead and buried it isn't in my manor, he thought. We'd have found her if it was. I wonder if Gideon talked to the others? He went to his desk and sat down heavily. "She isn't in a boat or a boat shed," he said aloud. "She isn't in a caravan. She isn't in an allotment shed. She isn't in a disused garage. She isn't in an empty house or flat." As he spoke he laid aside folder after folder with reports of investigations into all these places. "She isn't with any man who is known to be living alone. She isn't in a hotel or boarding house. So if she's in this division she's in a house where other people live. She isn't hiding for a joke, and she's no need to run away, so she must have been abducted. We've checked all the families with sons who are weak in the head, and whom we know need watching. So it must be someone we don't know—and most of the ones we don't know are families who've moved into the district in the last six months, say."

His face cleared as he lifted a telephone.

"Yes, sir?" His second-in-command answered promptly.

"I want someone to go round to the Town Clerk's office, see the Rating Officer and get a comprehensive list of all families known to have moved into the district in the past twelve months. Send others round to all estate agents to get lists of furnished houses or flats rented in the same period."

"Right, sir."

"Get it done quick," ordered Hellier.

He felt better when he rang off; at least he had started another line of inquiry, one it would have been easy to overlook.

Wanda Pierce was at the kitchen sink, preparing vegetables for lunch. David made a point of coming home to lunch, these days, although Mr. Lee didn't like it. In a way, it helped her. She knew what she was doing but did it mechanically. There was no relief from the mental agony she felt, no relief from the perpetual cross-examination of herself. She had *known* Geraldine was too easily flattered by men. She had *known* that she was extremely attractive and physically very well-developed for her age: she could pass for sixteen or seventeen anywhere.

"I tried to tell her. I tried all I knew," Wanda said drearily.

The words seemed to echo back at her from the empty garden.

She was alone. Mrs. Edmond would look in during the afternoon sometime, but she had her own family to look after. And none of the other neighbours came in often.

It was half-past eleven, and David would soon be back. Poor, useless, helpless David. If only he had some spirit! He should have left Lee years ago. *She* had always wanted to emigrate, to Australia preferably, but he had never had the necessary drive.

What would they do now?

At heart, she knew that only Geraldine had kept them together; left to herself she would have walked out on her husband years before.

Mr. Lee opened the door of David Pierce's office and found Pierce staring blankly out of the tiny window. He did not even look round as the door opened. Lee took the one stride needed to reach the desk.

"Pierce!" he barked.

Pierce started and looked round, wildly.

"What on earth are you doing? You take enough time off, these days, you should at least be giving your job your full attention when you *are* here."

Pierce didn't speak.

"Are the July stock-sheets ready yet?"

Pierce spoke slowly. "No. Not quite. They will be by middle afternoon."

"That won't be time enough," rapped Lee. "I want them in my office by two o'clock at the latest. Don't make any excuses."

He went out, closing the door with a snap.

Pierce turned to the loose-leaf ledger in

front of him, with its interminable lists of stationery stocks, all entered in his own small, neat handwriting. He had been doing this ever since he had left school, when he had taken over from an elderly clerk very soon after he had obtained the job.

The figures swam in front of him.

He looked at the big, round-faced clock on the opposite wall, and saw that it was nearly twelve o'clock. To get these lists ready by two would mean staying here throughout his lunch hour, and that would mean sending a message to tell Wanda that he wasn't coming home. He could imagine her expression when Mrs. Edmond told her. He knew that she almost despised him, and instead of the disaster drawing them closer together it seemed to be tearing them further apart. She couldn't help him and he couldn't help her. But he knew that she hated to be alone, and perhaps he *did* help a little by going home to lunch.

He stared at the clock.

He heard Wanda's voice in his imagination.

"*You ought to be out looking for her!*"

It was true; he ought to be.

Very slowly he stood up, put a marker

in the ledger, put on his jacket, and went through the small general office, where two girls were typing and another at the little switchboard was making entries in the day-book.

The girls paused in their typing as Pierce walked towards the outer door. He reached it, and turned round.

"Tell Mr. Lee that I will come back *after* my daughter is found."

He did not wait for an answer but went out, down the narrow stairs, out into the side street which led into the High Street and so to the river. He did not cross the bridge but walked to the police station. It was a quarter-past twelve when he asked for Hellier.

"What can I do for you, Mr. Pierce?" Hellier asked.

"You can give me something to do which may help me to find my daughter," Pierce said.

"Mr. Pierce, we are doing everything we possibly can. Amateur help will not—" Hellier began, and then he broke off, realising that once again he had said the wrong and cruel thing. He simply could not help being clumsy with words.

"But there must be something I can do. There *must* be," Pierce sounded desperate.

"But what about your work?" Hellier asked, shifting his ground weakly.

Stonily, Pierce answered: "I have left my job until Geraldine is found."

Awkwardly, Hellier dissembled. "Give me time to consider this, Mr. Pierce, and I will find the best way to use your services. Will you telephone me this afternoon?"

"I'm not on the telephone," Pierce replied. "Will you please send an officer to me with the message?" He turned and went out of the office, leaving Hellier staring after him.

Chapter Thirteen

PROMISE

Sir Jeremy Pilkington, tall and handsome, came down the gangway from the B.E.A. aircraft at London Airport with two beautiful young women in front of him and two equally beautiful young women behind. They were slender and exquisitely dressed, and as elegant as anyone presented by Dior and Jean Patou should be. At the entrance to the Customs hall a battery of at least a dozen cameras was turned towards them, several from television and the news reels. Trained to perfection, the young women posed without appearing to, were vivacious and attractively natural.

With the photographers were a dozen newspaper men.

"Just a moment, Sir Jeremy."

"Will you stand in the middle? Thank you, sir."

"If the blonde will change places with the tall brunette . . . Thank you."

"Just one more, sir, please."

"Will you tell us exactly where the parade is to be, Sir Jeremy?"

"Is it to be on the river?"

"Teddington?"

"Westminster?"

Sir Jeremy, obviously in his element, slipped his arm delicately round the brunette's waist.

"You'll know all about it in the morning," he promised. "I can tell you now that it will be the most magnificent show of furs, gowns, jewels and beautiful women ever staged in London. The spectacle not only of the year but of the decade." He spied his wife, on the fringe of the newspaper men and strode towards her, arms outstretched. "Hello, m'dear." He kissed her lightly on either cheek. "Lovely to see you, you ought to be *in* the show, not simply organising it."

"Will you do that again, sir?"

"Could you move a little closer, madam—*and* you madam. *And* you." The speaker motioned first to Lady Pilkington, then to the models.

Pilkington laughed. "That's enough now, gentlemen—more tomorrow." He inclined his head towards his wife. "Hugh here?"

"Yes, just coming."

"He can look after the models," said Pilkington. "Aren't they charming?"

"Most charming."

They both laughed.

A few minutes later Esmeralda was driving her husband out of the airport, while Hugh St. John, manager of the parade and renowned in London fashion circles, shepherded the models, allowed them to pose for a few more photographs, and then climbed after them into a big Chrysler.

Next to his wife, Pilkington was saying:

"What *is* all this about Alec Hobbs and his merry men, darling?"

"He's very put out because you didn't tell the police about the parade."

"But it would have spoiled the whole show if they'd started making preparations!"

"I told him that, but he didn't seem to think it important. Jeremy."

"Yes, m'dear?"

"I think *he* thinks there could be a robbery."

"Oh nonsense! Tosh! Rubbish!" Suddenly Pilkington seemed almost angry.

"Alec *can't* believe such balderdash. Didn't say anything to suggest it, did he?"

"Only that he was afraid of it."

"How did he hear about the parade?"

"Morris, the insurance man, told him."

"I'll have to talk to Morris," said Pilkington. "Secrecy is secrecy. *You're* not worried, are you?"

Esmeralda half-frowned. "I would hate anything to go wrong, darling."

"My God, so would I!" Pilkington sat back for a few seconds, then touched her hand—resting lightly on the wheel—as if he had forgotten that she was driving in the thick traffic of the Great West Road. "Perhaps it's as well Alec knows. The police won't let anything go wrong. As they know all about it, we needn't worry. Angel, you look absolutely *splendid*. Whenever I leave you for a few days I always wonder how I could have been such a fool."

Esmeralda laughed, but was obviously pleased.

Gideon, at the end of that day, was in one of his more dissatisfied moods. He felt as if he had been tied by hidden bonds to the desk, and this always irked him. Only now and again, as Commander, could he take any active share in an investigation; for the main part he could only guide the detectives in the field, from his office.

At the moment, except for the Pierce child, the coming parade, and the industrial diamonds problem, there were no major crimes going through. Summer was often a quiet period, which was just as well; school holidays meant holidays for policemen with their families as well as for criminals with theirs. But this was a quiet period in other ways, too. For years there had been the uncertainty about Lemaitre and his, Gideon's deputy; and there had been a strong move to promote him, Gideon, to the post of Assistant Commissioner. All of these things had helped to create pressures and tensions, and Gideon heaved a great sigh of relief when they had passed. Yet the truth was that he missed them.

Now that he had been on the river there was no excuse to go out into the Divisions, and this made him feel restless. He had given all the thought he could to the Pierce case; in fact there was nothing he could do which Hellier couldn't do at least as well.

A tap at the door made Gideon look up from his desk, and as he did so the door opened, and Hobbs came in, closing it carefully behind him. In some contradictory way Hobbs's calm and unquestioned efficiency both took a load off Gideon's shoulders and, at the same time, added to his restlessness.

"What's on, Alec?"

"Nothing new of any significance." Hobbs said that as if it were routine. "I've just heard that Pilkington is back from Paris, and has promised the press a statement by tomorrow morning."

"That's what we expected, isn't it?"

"Yes—" Hobbs paused, and then added: "George."

"Yes?"

"Prescott and Roswell worried me."

" 'Big River Robbery', you mean?"

"Yes."

"Got under my skin, too," Gideon admitted. "It obviously sprang to everybody's mind." He did not add that it had also drawn attention from the waterproof bag story; no one had been particularly interested in that, although each had examined the bag.

"*Is* there a way it could be staged?"

"Meaning, is Worby over-confident?" Gideon pursed his lips. "Worby's always inclined to be, of course. In this case—I don't know. He's quite right in his assertion that it's difficult to start anything quickly on the water."

"Yes." Hobbs frowned. "Yes, I suppose so. Or under it."

"But not above it," said Gideon slowly.

Hobbs stared.

"Above?"

Gideon frowned. "I don't know what protection those jewels will have, but if they *were* all in one place, if someone aboard *did* steal them and get them on to the deck, say, and if—" he hesitated, feeling that the possibility which had entered his head was too ridiculous to utter, then went on—"and if a helicopter was hovering, ostensibly to take photographs, but with someone on board ready to signal when it was worth swooping down and using a grab—"

Hobbs gave a low-pitched whistle.

"Great River Robbery, Method One!"

"I know it sounds absurd." Gideon sounded almost apologetic.

"But it *could* happen," said Hobbs excitedly. "One swoop, and a crate could be plucked off the deck, and dropped beside a waiting car or van almost anywhere in London, within a few minutes of the robbery."

Gideon began to rub his chin.

"It *isn't* absurd," Hobbs argued. "And I wouldn't like to take any chances," he added.

"Nor would I," growled Gideon. "We've two clear days before the damned thing starts."

"Nearly three," Hobbs corrected. "It starts at six-thirty, to miss the worst of the rush-hour. From what I saw of the *River Belle* they'll be working right through the night to get the *décor* finished. Care to look over it yourself?"

"No, I'll leave that part to you. But I'll drive home along the Embankment and see what they're doing on the pier."

In fact, there was very little to see, except an army of workmen on the pier and on the river boats, as well as several tradesmen's vans parked nearby. A Superintendent of the Division was talking to a uniformed Inspector, obviously about parking and re-routing traffic. Gideon didn't stop, but raised a hand to them. Just beyond the pier the *Belle Casino* was gay with bunting, but practically no one was aboard: gaming seldom started in earnest until after dark.

When he turned into the gate of his home in Harrington Street, Gideon heard the first theme of a Beethoven Concerto, being played in his front room. So Penelope was home and practising. Bless the girl, she spent every moment she could at the piano. He let himself in as the majestic notes rolled out, and for some absurd reason almost tiptoed past the half-open door. There was no one in the kitchen or the living-room, and he wondered if Kate were out. There was no note. Suddenly the piano playing stopped and Penelope came hurrying.

"Is that you, Daddy? Oh, *there* you are!"

Penelope was twenty-two, and the least attractive of the Gideon daughters, but she had a merry expression in her brown eyes, a snub nose, and nice lips. She was the most vivacious of the family. Giving Gideon a hug, she went on: "Mummy's gone over to Pru's and is going to stay the night . . . There's a casserole in the oven . . . Neil's out until midnight, and Priscilla will be late too."

"So that leaves you and me," Gideon said.

"Leaves you," said Penelope, briskly. "I've a rehearsal, and a date afterwards. I just waited to say hello-goodbye."

"Hello, goodbye," Gideon said ruefully.

He ate the contents of the casserole, and a large slice of apple tart, then went into the living-room and switched on the television. Almost at once there was the sound of shooting, sure herald of a Western. He picked up the evening newspaper and half-watched the screen while skimming the headlines, read a small paragraph about the Pierces, another about the infanticide, an inside page story of the finding of Tom Argyle-Morris's body. The Yard wasn't getting anywhere with any of the main inquiries, he thought despondently, that must be why he was feeling so depressed.

He put the paper down and, despite the

figures cavorting across the screen, began to doze. It was pleasant and comfortable. Then, suddenly, the telephone bell disturbed him. He was so near sleep that he wondered, at first, what it was; then how long it had been ringing. If it was the Yard it would go on and on, if it was a family call it would probably stop ringing before he reached it.

It didn't stop, and he lifted the receiver. "Gideon."

"George, you were quite right to ask me to keep a weather-eye open for Micklewright." It was Worby speaking. "One of his sisters-in-law has just phoned me. She says he's drunk as a lord and swearing that he's going to kill his wife. Did you know she'd gone off with another man?"

Gideon sat in the back of a car which had been sent from the Yard and was being driven along the Embankment. Now that it was dark, the *Belle Casino* was ablaze with light, and across the river, Battersea Park Pleasure Gardens, lively survivor of the 1951 Exhibition, was gay and gaudy with lights of a dozen colours, reflecting with rare beauty on the dark water. Gideon was aware of these things, but thinking only of Micklewright and his wife.

Why hadn't he made Micklewright talk? The man must have been at breaking point for days, if not for weeks. With a little more effort he could have been persuaded to tell the whole story.

Self-reproach was a waste of time, though.

Micklewright was believed to be somewhere between his own home in Stepney, and the flat where his wife was known to be living, in Greenwich, and Worby had alerted the Division which covered Greenwich.

"According to his sister-in-law, he's twice been forcibly restrained from attacking his wife," Worby had reported.

"Is the wife's place being protected?"

"He won't get through, George, don't worry."

"I hope not," Gideon had said, grimly.

Now, as the car sped along through London's night, all the other factors went in and out of his mind. There was Micklewright's personal problem, which explained so much. There was the fact that tension and too much whisky were stopping him from doing his job well. There was the fact that he had upset Van Hoorn. There was the fact that he would have to be taken off the inquiry, and it was always a bad thing to put a new man in charge halfway through a case. There was another, in some ways the most important factor, of all: if Micklewright did reach his wife and attack her it would be a major sensation, and would do great harm to the public image of the police. That image was better now than it had been for some time, but it needed comparatively little to blur it. There might be no fairness in a situation by which one policeman's personal tragedy could affect the reputation of the entire Force, but it could and, if this got out, it would.

"Have the press learned about this, yet?" he had asked Worby.

"Not as far as I know, George."

The best way to Greenwich by night was across London Bridge and then along the Old Kent Road through New Cross and Deptford. The Tower Bridge was vivid in floodlights. Gideon had only to turn his head to see the floodlit walls of the Tower itself. The road, which seemed deserted, was poorly lit. Every moment he expected a message by radio, but none came. At last the car drew up alongside another police car at the end of a tree-lined avenue. Two men came forward: first, Joe Mullivan Superintendent in charge of Q.R. Division, then the last man Gideon had expected, Old Man River Singleton.

Joe Mullivan, big and massive, one of the few men in the Force who was bigger than Gideon, opened the door.

"Any sign of him?" Gideon demanded at once.

"Not near here, sir."

"Anywhere?" growled Gideon.

"We've had a report that an acquaintance of his saw him in a pub in Deptford half an hour ago."

Gideon frowned. "Does his wife know what's happening?"

"No," Mullivan said.

"She ought to be warned," put in Singleton gruffly. "That's my opinion, sir."

He glared almost defiantly at Gideon.

"What are you doing here?" demanded Gideon.

"They're both old friends of mine, sir.

I could see this marriage was heading for the rocks years ago. I want to go and see Clara but the Superintendent refused to allow me to go up to her place until you arrived. I'd like your permission, sir."

Chapter Fourteen

THE MURDEROUS POLICEMAN

In the shadows cast by the street lamps were several detectives, their faces pale shapes, their bodies dark. Beyond Gideon was the driver, in front of him Mullivan and Singleton—and Singleton was obviously fighting to retain his composure. Here was a case where the human, emotional side of a policeman was getting on top of his official side. A couple came round a corner, walking briskly as they turned into the street, slowing down when they saw the cars and the men. All of these things flickered through Gideon's mind. There was more than enough to worry about without Singleton, but the wrong attitude towards him now could do a lot of harm in several ways. Even in the few seconds while he deliberated, Gideon saw a hardening of defiance in Singleton's craggy face, in full expectancy of a refusal.

"It's a long time since I've seen Clara

Micklewright," Gideon said. "I think I'll come along with you."

The defiance, the half-formed resentment, vanished into thin air.

"That's going to *make* her take it seriously!" Singleton was almost jubliant.

"I hope so. Superintendent—" Gideon turned to Mullivan—"What's the position?"

"The house is watched back and front, sir, and we've men in the gardens of neighbouring houses, even got two men on the roof opposite."

"With long-beam lamps?"

"Yes, sir."

"Good." Gideon turned and walked along the street of tall, terraced houses with Singleton, who suddenly seemed tongue-tied.

"Anything about the Pierce girl, sir?" he asked at last.

"Not yet."

"Hell of a thing to happen."

"Yes," Gideon said. "And this is a hell of a thing to happen to Micklewright. You say you've been expecting it?"

"For years," answered Singleton. "It was one of those misfit marriages from the beginning. God knows what Clara ever saw in Mick. Easy to understand what he sees in her, though."

"Much younger than he is, isn't she?"

"Fifteen years. She was *too* young, I suppose. Hero-worshipped him, in a way—remember when he won that life-saving medal?"

"Yes," said Gideon, turning his mind back to the time when Micklewright had plunged off Chelsea Bridge to rescue two children who had fallen from a pleasure boat.

"They met about that time. Er—I'm not talking out of place, sir, am I?"

"Not a bit."

As Gideon spoke, they reached a gate where a man stood on guard and another was close by. Bushes grew in the small garden beyond, and whitened steps led up to a dark front door. There was a light over the door and a light at a high window. On one side of the porch were several bell pushes, each with card underneath; Singleton pressed the top button as he went on:

"Everything was all right for a few years. They had one child, a girl—but she died at the age of six. She'd held them together. Mick buried himself in his work but Clara hadn't anything to bury herself in, so she got a job as a model, and—well, she's enough to make most men lose their heads."

Gideon asked, rather grimly: "She lived it up, did she?"

"Yes, sir—but she didn't let Mick down. Not for years, anyhow. She kept their home clean as a new pin, and she's one of the best cooks I know. He didn't seem to mind the rest."

"Did he know what was going on?"

"Oh, he *knew* all right."

"Then what's this trouble about?"

Singleton pressed the bell-push again, and said:

"She asked him for a divorce, and that changed things. A year ago, that was. She met this chap she's living with, Jonathan Wild, and fell in love. They wanted to marry, but Mick wouldn't go along with divorce. He said he'd shut his eyes to an affair and wouldn't make any trouble provided she stayed in his house, as his wife. Didn't make any demands on her—what the hell is happening?" He rang the bell again. "They usually press the button upstairs and the door opens."

"Sure they're in?"

"There's a light on at their window."

"Do you come here often?"

"Once most weeks," answered Singleton. "As a matter of fact I knew Jonathan before—"

"Who's there?" a man asked from the other side of the door.

Singleton raised his voice.

"It's Jake and a friend."

"Hang on a moment." There was a sound of a chain being taken out of its channel, then a creak as the door opened. The light from the hall was behind the man who opened the door, but a street light shone on to his lean, hatchet-like face. Gideon had an impression of an over-poweringly handsome man with shining dark eyes. "Hello, Jake," he said. "Who's your friend?"

"Commander Gideon," Singleton answered.

Wild's eyes widened almost ludicrously.

"This *is* an honour. Do come in." He stood aside for the others to enter, then closed the door. "I suppose you've come because Mick is on the rampage again," he added. He said "Mick" with a kind of friendly familiarity which surprised Gideon.

"How did you know?" Singleton asked quickly.

"Jessie telephoned," answered Wild.

"Clara's sister," Singleton interpolated.

"And I thought I'd better not release the street door from upstairs," Wild went on. He kept his voice low as he led the way up a flight of narrow stairs, which curved round at a landing. The ceilings were high, the walls dark, the landing lights dim. "How much does the Commander know?"

"You can speak quite freely," Gideon said.

"Then I will. He did get in once, three weeks ago, and really scared Clara. Until then she didn't take his threats seriously, but she does now. Everything's all right until he hits the bottle. Then it can be hell. I—*My God*, what's that?"

Across his words from high above their heads came a high-pitched scream.

"Don't!" a woman cried, "No, no no!"

"He's up there!" cried Wild, and he

sprang forward as if there were springs in the heels of his boots.

The woman screamed again, in wild terror.

"Micklewright!" roared Gideon in a tremendous voice. "Stop that!"

Then Wild tripped on the stairs.

As he tripped and fell, he banged his head heavily on the wall, grunted, and sprawled down. Gideon was just behind him, the woman was screaming, a door on the next landing opened and a man appeared, calling out ineffectually. Gideon dodged as Wild slipped down another stair, then sprang over him, holding tight to the banister.

Upstairs, a door slammed.

Gideon took the stairs two at a time, swung round another landing, then, in the dim light, saw a door at the next one, shut and dark. Reaching the door, he tried the handle and thrust hard, but found it would not budge. Drawing back three feet, he hurled himself against it, his great weight making it creak and groan. He drew back again. The screaming had stopped. He had an awful fear that he was too late, and summoned still greater strength for his second attempt.

With a deafening crash the door swung open.

In front of him, back towards him, Micklewright had his hands round his wife's neck. She was pressed against the wall, her head held tight against it, her eyes huge and staring, her mouth open, her teeth bared.

Gideon swept his right arm round and struck Micklewright a tremendous buffet on the side of the head. Micklewright swayed and his grip on his wife's throat slackened. Gideon hit him again. This time his hands fell and he staggered, struck a chair, and crashed to the floor. His wife, hands at her throat, was beginning to slide down the wall. Even in that strange and tense situation, Gideon noticed the beautiful shape of her hands, and the soft pink of the lacquer on her nails. He thrust an arm round her waist and drew her away from the wall, as Singleton said:

"I'll look after her, sir."

Seeing a couch on one side of the room, Gideon carried the woman over to it, laid her down gently, and drew back. She was breathing harshly, painfully. Singleton, pushing in front of him, knelt beside the couch and began to loosen the waistband of her skirt.

Wild came in, limping.

Micklewright began to claw himself to his feet.

Wild glanced at him without expression, then hurried towards the couch.

Singleton looked up at him. "Turn the bed down, get hot water bottles, then hot coffee," he ordered.

"Right." Wild turned away, glanced at Micklewright again, then went out of the room. He said something under his breath; it sounded like "thanks." He disappeared. Gideon took Micklewright by the arm and held him steady. His eyes were bleary and bloodshot, his nose was red and shiny, but his cheeks were the colour of pastry and his lips looked faintly blue. He kept moistening them and touching the side of his face as if wondering why it stung so much. His gaze did not focus properly, and he began to sway to and fro. Gideon felt a mingled disgust and compassion.

And he began to face up to the things that would have to be done.

First—get Micklewright to a police

station; next, sober him up—no, next have a police surgeon and an independent doctor examine him, *then* sober him up. Get a psychiatrist to examine him, tonight. Charge him with attempted murder—

Must he?

He could charge him with common assault.

No, Gideon thought, that would be impossible. Too many people had heard of his threats, dozens had probably heard him tonight. The neighbour on the landing below had heard everything and may have seen much. There could be no white-washing. God damn it! Gideon suddenly roared within himself, there shouldn't *be* any thought of whitewashing! What was the matter with him? The charge would have to be attempted murder. And as soon as Micklewright was at the station some-one would tell the press and tomorrow the court would be crammed full to overflowing.

As for the evening paper headlines—

Again, but with less vehemence, he thought: Oh, hell, what's the matter with me? He *did* it. In another two minutes his wife would have been dead. He had a brainstorm while he was drunk.

In fact, it wasn't going to be as simple as that; but at least from the police point of view it was nothing like as bad as a charge of corruption.

Singleton stepped to his side.

"She's all right now," he said.

"Thank God."

"And thank you, sir. If you hadn't got that door down when you did—"

"Where was Micklewright hiding?" Gideon asked.

"As far as I can find out, sir, he forced a downstairs window, came through the ground floor flat while the family was watching television, and let himself into the hall. Seems to have been hiding in a landing cupboard for a long time—before the alarm was raised, I would think. The cupboard stinks of whisky and there's an empty bottle on the floor. God knows what he meant to do, but he was crafty enough to stay in hiding."

"Awaiting his chance, I suppose," Gideon said.

"George . . . George . . . " Micklewright began to mumble "George . . . Gee . . . *Gee-Gee*! Commander." He drew himself up to an unsteady attention "'Evening, sir."

There were other men here now, including Mullivan. Micklewright looked at them all as if puzzled, turned back to Gideon, and said thickly: "Commander Gideon, sir!"

Gideon turned to Mullivan. "Take him, will you. Get our doctor and another G.P. and ask them to call a psychiatrist. Don't charge him until I come—I'll be with you soon."

"Right, sir," said Mullivan. "Are *you* all right?"

"Yes. Why shouldn't I be?"

"Er—" Mullivan grunted, turned to Micklewright and gripped him lightly just above the elbow. "Come on, Mick," he said, his voice surprisingly gentle.

Gideon moved across to a chair and sat down, a little annoyed with himself because he felt so very weary. Almost as soon as he relaxed, Jonathan Wild came towards him, limping, carrying a bottle of whisky in one hand and a glass and a soda syphon on a tray. He was smiling twistedly, but Gideon's impression of a remarkably handsome man was stronger than ever.

"Will you have a drink?"

"Thanks."

Wild poured out a generous tot.

"Soda?"

"Fill it up, please."

The soda water gurgled and fizzed.

"Thanks." Gideon lifted the glass.

"Commander, I can't hope to tell you how—how grateful I am."

"You don't need to try."

"But I *shall* try," said Wild. "And another thing, I would like you to know that I—" he hesitated—"that I really do love her."

Gideon thought: Yes, I can see that he does. Aloud, he said: "I'm very glad she's all right."

"And I want you to know that I hope it will be possible not to charge Mick."

"Mick" again.

Gideon frowned. "Assault is assault."

"He's a sick man, Commander. Some will say I helped to make him sick. All I want you to know is that if there is any way I can help him now, I will."

"Mr. Wild," Gideon said, "we aren't going to be vindictive. You can be sure of that."

Wild's lips seemed to curl.

"But the law is the law and because he's an upholder of it will have to be punished with the utmost vigour. Yes, I see. Don't you sometimes hate the law, Commander?"

After a few moments reflection Gideon drank again and then replied: "If you want to invoke the aid of the law for Superintendent Micklewright, the best way is to get a lawyer who really knows what he's doing. If the lawyer is briefed before he's called to the police station, it will help." He finished his drink and went on: "I needed that!"

"Another, Commander?"

"No, thanks."

There was a long pause, then Wild gave a jerky little nod, and said: "I'll do just what you recommend."

Chapter Fifteen

THE THREE MEN

At about the time that Gideon was drinking his whisky and soda on the south side of the river, three men were sitting round a table in an apartment on the north side, less than a quarter of a mile from Scotland Yard. One of these was the big man with the guttural voice who had been in the disused shed at the Royal Docks. He wore a dinner jacket which was rather too small for him, and a big-winged bow tie; the unlit cigar jutting from his lips looked like an extension of his face. Opposite him in a high-backed armchair was a very much smaller man with a curiously baby-like face, smooth and peach-pink, and fair, silky hair. He was also wearing a dinner jacket.

The third man was Hugh St. John, Sir Jeremy Pilkington's chief *aide*.

St. John wore the grey suit with green flecks that he had worn at the airport that afternoon. He was good-looking in an un-English way, with thick dark hair rising high from his forehead, a sallow complexion, full lips and a long, down-curved nose. There was something very finicky about his movements and his attitudes; sitting there he gave an impression of impatience, of disdain for his two companions.

"I want to know exactly what happened in Paris," the big man said.

"I don't know what happened in Paris," St. John replied.

"You are paid to get the information."

"Holmann, I am sure St. John is being wise not to claim to know everything," interpolated the man with the baby face.

"That's right," said St. John. "I get paid for telling you what I know. Not what you would like to know. I'm not sure that I get paid enough." There was a supercilious expression on his face as he glanced from the big man to the small man. "What do you think, Morro?"

The baby-faced man said: "You will be well paid when we have the jewels."

"And if you don't get the jewels?"

"None of us will be well paid," murmured Morro.

"What are you talking about—we are going to get them," said Holmann. His English was good but rather precise and with a momentary hesitation before certain words. "That is, if you do your job."

St. John leaned back in his chair. "The jewels will be on the *River Belle*. The value will be approximately half-a-million pounds. They will be insured for seven hundred and fifty thousand pounds, at Lloyd's. In all there will be seventy-two different pieces—twelve models will wear six pieces each. The models will be given the jewellery only two or three minutes before they appear before the guests. Cheap costume jewellery will be used at rehearsals, including the dress rehearsal an hour before the real event occurs. Each piece, with a numbered tag, will be taken out of the portable fire-proof safe and given straight to Gentian, who will pin it on to the model and will take it off when she has finished. An insurance representative, two Securial officers, and I, will be present all the time. I will take the jewels out of the safe and hand them to Gentian, and he will give them back to me to put back into the safe."

He paused, to sip from a big brandy glass.

Morro murmured: "It is very thorough."

"It must be thorough," Holmann said. "This is good, I agree."

St. John gave a wry, thin-lipped smile. "I am glad you think so. There will be spotlights shining on each model in the bar where she is given the jewels. The safe will be under a spot-light all the time. The jewels will be in the full view of at least six people every moment, and for most of the time in full view of hundreds—including some very important policemen."

"What is that?" exclaimed Morro.

"Of Scotland Yard?" asked Holmann.

"Pilkington has invited Commander Gideon and his wife, Deputy Commander Hobbs and a friend, and two officials from the Thames Division," St. John informed them. "There will be Customs officers as well as Thames Division officers on board all the time."

"Naturally," Holmann was quite unflustered.

"The portable safe will be locked by the Securial officers and kept on board overnight, with a four man armed guard on duty," continued St. John. "Police, Customs and Securial officers will escort it from the bank to the *River Belle* and back late on the Tuesday evening. The Customs will check item by item on Tuesday evening at the bank and it will then be collected by the different jewel merchants who are lending it for display on Wednesday morning."

Morro was looking earnestly at Holmann.

"It is very thorough, isn't it? Our only opportunity to get the jewels will be as they are brought to the river, or as they are taken from it."

"There will be at least twenty Securial men at the landing stage and on the Embankment, and probably twice as many police," St. John answered, and when neither of the others spoke he went on: "Now do you see why I doubt if we'll get the jewels, Holmann?"

"You are paid to provide information," Holmann said, drawing at the unlit cigar. "Now to consider whether we shall get them. Or *how* we shall get them."

"I don't think you can," St. John retorted. "That's why I wonder whether a thousand pounds is enough for the risk I'm taking. If you make an attempt, and fail—"

"I do not fail," said Holmann, harshly. "Have you a plan of the ship?"

"I'm no draughtsman, but I've some rough drawings."

"Did I not understand that Gentian had drawings of the interior of the ship so that he could perfect the *décor*?"

"He has only one copy."

"There are such things as cameras."

"Oh, no," said St. John "I'm not going to take that much of a risk. I'll pass on what I learn in the way of business but I won't do anything which will point to me if I were seen or caught."

"St. John—" Morro began, nervously.

"It is a reasonable attitude," said Holmann, unexpectedly. "We do not want him caught any more than he does himself. Show me these rough drawings, please."

St. John lifted his flat, black brief-case from the side of his chair, unzipped it, and took out a folder. He opened this and handed it over the table to Holmann, then looked at the brandy decanter.

"Please," Morro said. He pushed the decanter closer to St. John, who first selected a cigar, clipped the end, cut it, and then helped himself to more brandy. Holmann was scrutinising the drawings which were in dark pencil and had a number of annotations and indications of dimensions. He looked from one page to another—there were four in all—and finally back at St. John. He was smiling faintly; the curve to his lips made him look vaguely like a tiger.

"These are good," he announced.

St. John bowed sardonically. "They're the best I could do."

"How did you do them?"

"They were done for Securial, and I kept a copy."

"Good," repeated Holmann. "These sizes, are they accurate? Especially the width of the doors . . ."

He asked questions, searchingly, most of which St. John was able to answer. Holmann seemed even more satisfied when he had finished. He placed a pudgy hand on St. John's shoulder, then took out a fat wallet and selected a number of ten pound notes. He placed these in front of St. John.

"I hope you will feel better rewarded with this extra money," he said.

Without counting the notes, St. John picked them up and nodded.

"Thank you."

"And you are not likely to be called on for any other service until after the river parade," Holmann added.

St. John stood up, looking intently into his eyes. They were slightly yellowish, with an outer fringe of green round the pupil, the lids sallow, with tiny folds of flesh about them. St. John did not voice any questions but plenty were in his expression.

"I will come to the lift with you," said Morro.

Again, St. John nodded.

A few minutes later he stepped in a black Jaguar 3½ litre parked in the forecourt of the block of modern flats. A doorman stood and watched him, indifferently. There was a hint of rain in the air but not enough to call for windscreen wipers. St. John drove towards the Embankment, with Victoria Station behind him. It was very dark until he drew near the *River Belle* and the *Belle Casino* over each of which was a glow of light. He parked fairly near the pier and looked across at the lights of the pleasure gardens, then walked past two policemen towards the gangway leading to the pier. Three couples, the women beautifully dressed, came up from the casino. Two doormen were at the pier, another man stood on the gangway leading to the *River Belle*. Lights shone all over the old boat, two floodlights on the bows were slowly being swivelled round, and there was a sound of hammering.

St. John went into the main salon.

Gentian and two girls, all wearing pale mauve pants and primrose yellow shirts, were draping the windows with gold-coloured fabrics. Gentian had a mouthful of pins and was mumbling:

"How about the height, dear . . . Not *on* the floor, but not more than half-an-inch above it . . . Is that right?" He put in a number of pins, then looked across, saw St. John and widened his eyes in surprise. He took the pins out of his mouth carefully.

"What are we doing wrong now? If anything?"

St. John raised his eyebrows. "I didn't come to see what you were doing wrong, I wanted to find out if anything was going right."

The girls exchanged meaning glances. Gentian made no comment.

"What chance is there of being ready on time?" asked St. John.

"If we don't get any more interruptions we shall be ahead of time," retorted Gentian.

"*And* if we work all night," said one of the girls.

St. John ignored her. "Has Sir Jeremy been here this evening?" he asked Gentian.

"No."

St. John nodded, and went out. As he disappeared and while he was within ear-shot, one of the girls said feelingly:

"How I *hate* that man."

"He probably doesn't like you very much," Gentian remarked. "Now, the other window, dear . . ."

St. John strolled on to the deck, looked about him, seeing the beauty of the lights reflected from the Embankment and the bridges on the dark water, then crossed to the landing stage and walked towards the *Belle Casino*. The men on duty stood aside. He went in and sauntered about the crowded room. The two big roulette tables were besieged by well-dressed men and women, the blackjack nearly as crowded. Two red-headed girls and several long-haired youths were at the craps table, the girls giggling, one of them shooting the dice. In a far corner two tables of poker seemed to be part of a different world.

The cashier was near the craps table, and the office was behind it.

St. John went to the door of the office and tapped. It was opened after a few seconds by a hard-faced, middle-aged woman who stood to one side. An elderly, grey-haired man was at a pedestal desk, with a safe behind him.

"Well?" he said.

St. John laid the money which Holmann had paid him on the desk. The man took it, counted it, and handed him five notes back. Then he opened a drawer and took out an I.O.U. for four hundred and fifty pounds, signed by St. John. He handed this across.

St. John picked a book of matches from a big glass ashtray and set light to a corner of the paper and watched it burn. In everything he did there was an air of calculated insult.

"St. John," the man said, "don't ask me for money again."

"I won't ask you for anything again," St. John said. He nodded and went out. The two red-heads were on their way to the powder room, and both glanced at him. He went to the roulette table, waited for ten minutes, then bought fifty pounds' worth of counters and placed them on Number 7, straight. The croupier pushed other counters about, no one spoke, smoke was very thick. The croupier called:

"*Rein ne va plus*," and paused momentarily before he spun the wheel. The soft whirring of the running ball sounded clearly against the background noises from the rest of the room, then slowed down to a hushed murmur.

The ball almost settled in twenty-nine, and then went over seven into twenty-eight.

St. John turned away. Two or three of the officials watched him thoughtfully. He spoke to no one but, outside, paused to take another look at the still surface of the river before moving up to his car.

Another car, a red Mini Minor, started

up just ahead of him and turned out into the Jaguar's wake. At the wheel was a young man, by his side a girl with a lot of blonde hair which fell almost to her shoulders.

At the Greenwich Police Station, Gideon was saying to Mullivan: "It will have to be attempted murder."

"Yes, I know."

"Wait for an hour," Gideon advised. "You may find he'll be legally represented by then. How is he?"

"Honestly, sir, I don't know whether he's still blind drunk or fooling. He doesn't seem to make any sense at all. Our doctor thinks he's drunk, the other man thinks it may be a nervous collapse."

For the first time, Gideon seemed to brighten.

"If they prove that, it could help," he said. "Hell of a job, whatever happens. Is Singleton here?"

"No, but he left a note for you," Mullivan replied, and handed Gideon a sealed envelope. Gideon did not open it until he was in the back of the car being driven home to Fulham. Then he read:

"Just want to say thank you very much, sir."

His spirits lifted a little, and on the way home he was able to relax enough to reflect, a little sententiously, on the fact that just as two hours ago he had had no idea of what was in Micklewright's mind, so at this moment he had no idea of what was being planned anywhere in London.

Was there a plot to raid the River Parade, for instance? *Was* there a big organisation behind the industrial diamond losses? *Was* Geraldine Pierce alive, and if so, what ordeal had she suffered? What was going on in the minds of her parents? What other men, driven to drink and despair by the loss of their wives, might go berserk tonight? How many practised criminals were out on their furtive work, how many people were committing a crime for the first time in their lives?

There was no end to the questions.

And there was no end to the secrets in this vast, sleeping city through which the wide river flowed so silently and mysteriously, burdened with ships and their cargoes moving to and from so many parts of the world.

Chapter Sixteen

RING MARK

Police Constable Charles Addis of the Thames Division had spent the first ten years of his working life, from fifteen to twenty-five, at sea as a merchant sailor. He had obtained his master's certificate, then had met the girl he had wanted to marry and no longer desired to leave London for months at a time. So he had joined the Metropolitan Police force, going immediately to the Thames Division and soon becoming a member of the crew of a patrol with Chief Inspector Singleton in charge, and Police Sergeant Tidy, ten years his senior, as second-in-command.

Addis lay long awake that night, his wife Elsie sleeping soundly beside him.

Everything was fine between him and Elsie—even though she didn't like it when he was on night duty and had a secret longing for him to leave the Force. But this he didn't know. Their first child was on the way, which delighted him and rather frightened Elsie. That night, however, he wasn't thinking about Elsie or the child, he was thinking about that packet of industrial diamonds.

He had hooked it out of the water; had been the second man to touch it. He had a proprietorial attitude towards it—this was *his* case. He knew everything which had been done, had taken Micklewright and the Dutchman with the wide shoulders on a beat from Greenwich to Hammersmith and had heard them talking freely. Van Hoorn was sure there was a big organisation at work, and that the packet he, Addis, had found had been one of many. Micklewright had doubted this but had been prepared to look.

Short of searching every ship which came in from the Western European ports, there was nothing else to be done. Van Hoorn had said to Micklewright only the previous day:

"It is possible, surely, to have the Customs search every ship."

"Give us proof or even a good reason, and they will," Micklewright had said.

So Addis, taking a chance, had talked to

an officer of the Water Guard, a man whom he knew slightly.

"Search every ship?" the Customs man had echoed. "You'll be lucky! It's a filthy job, takes a hell of a time—you ever crawled along the propeller shaft and got yourself covered with stinking grease, mate? And we wouldn't do it unless there was a hell of a good reason. Do you know what you're asking? With those freighters we might get fifty in a day! Fifty! Have a heart!"

And he was right.

"Besides," the Customs man had added, "they could be in a waterproof container, made to float, and tossed overboard in the Estuary, miles before Tilbury even, and picked up by a small boat. If you suggest this lark, chum, you'll be the best hated man in the Water Guard."

He had laughed and slapped Addis on the shoulders.

Addis could almost feel the force of the blow as he lay there.

To make such a search even for one day *would* be impossible, unless there was a very powerful motive. It would require thousands of men from the Force, Customs,

City and Port of London police. If a couple of coppers were bumped off, now—

"Don't be a bloody fool!" he muttered, half serious, half laughing at himself.

It would need that kind of sensation. All the same, there must be a way of cracking this problem.

He began to think of the packet, picturing it in his mind's eye. There had been that round mark on one side, the kind of mark that was caused by rubber feet standing on a plain surface. He had a typewriter which made the same kind of mark on paper, even on a table. Could that have any significance? The packet was at Scotland Yard, trust them to hog everything there was in the way of evidence. But there were some photographs of it at the Wapping station.

It was nearly dawn—five o'clock, he guessed. He turned over and looked at the bedside clock; it was ten to five. He could lie awake no longer; he'd had it. He got out of bed cautiously, and, thank goodness, Elsie didn't stir. It wouldn't surprise her if he were gone when she woke, he was due off soon after seven, anyhow—always waking himself rather than putting on the alarm early enough to wake Elsie. He dressed very quietly, went downstairs and made himself some tea, then set off for the Wapping High Street Station.

His wife heard the front door close.

She stretched right across the bed, pulled his pillow under her, and dozed off again, slightly resentful.

Why did he always have to wake her up?

Perhaps if they had twin beds it would be better.

The night duty men were still at the Wapping High Street Station when Addis arrived. The man on duty in the Chief Inspector's room made the inevitable crack: "Your wife kick you out, Charlie?" He went out, through the boat shed where one of the small patrol boats and the Superintendent's launch were being serviced. Round the propeller shaft to the patrol boat was a coil of thick steel.

"Got to take the prop shaft off to put *that* right," a mechanic complained.

"My heart bleeds for you," Addis remarked, and went out towards the pier. Here the river was wide and smooth. On the far side were the warehouses and wharves; not far off were the big piles of timber in the Surrey Docks. Two lighters, each towing four barges, were following each other up river. Not far off, a ship's siren blasted—either as the ship arrived or when it was about to leave. A customs cutter went past, busily. Over on the far side, in the roads, were at least a dozen barges: on one of them was a man. Addis turned away from the water, which put new life into him, and looked into the Inspector's room again.

"Anyone seen the man on the barges at Elbow Roads?"

"Fred went over and had a look. He's a Rodent Officer, they've got some rats over there," the duty man replied. "They used to call 'em rat catchers."

"That's when they caught rats!"

Addis went into the C.I.D. room, where the photographs were pinned on the wall next to a notice about a Police Federation meeting. He stood studying them intently. There were six—one from each side of the packet, one from each edge, which all looked the same. The faint ring showed up more clearly in the photograph, because of the way the flash had been positioned. Addis began to frown. He had seen something like this before. It was like the ring impression made by a suction cap. Mines were stuck on to the hulls of ships with small round suction caps.

His heart began to beat very fast, and he could hardly wait for Old Man River to come in.

Gideon was up next morning before Penelope or Malcolm, grumbled to himself while he made some tea, decided to breakfast at the Yard, and was there before eight o'clock. The night duty men were just going, all with that rather worn look that nightworkers always had, the day duty men were coming in, with some of the office staff. It was a bright morning, much more crisp than yesterday. He rang for a messenger, and an old, retired constable now on the civil staff came in.

"Bacon and eggs for a hungry man, Jim!"

"Yes, Mr. Gideon. Coffee as usual?"

"Everything as usual," Gideon said, reflecting that it must be three months since he had last had breakfast at the Yard.

He went into Hobbs's office, but no new reports had reached Hobbs yet, not even about Micklewright. It was strange but he, Gideon, wanted to shut out the recollection of what had happened last night, and even resisted a temptation to telephone Mullivan.

The messenger brought in an enormous breakfast.

"Thought you could manage three eggs, Mr. Gideon."

"How right you were!" Gideon knew that he was being over-hearty, but knew also that this was the best way to treat this particular messenger. He watched the man spread a white cloth over a small table and lay knives and forks and everything needed for breakfast. Then the messenger said:

"Is it true about Mr. Micklewright, sir?"

Gideon looked at him levelly.

"What have you heard, Jim?"

"That he's been charged with the attempted murder of his wife, sir."

"I'm afraid it is true," Gideon admitted, quietly.

"I couldn't be more sorry," the messenger said. "A very kind gentleman, Mr. Micklewright."

"So it's all over the Yard," Gideon remarked.

"Proper buzzing with it, sir."

Gideon nodded, sat down and gradually began to concentrate on his breakfast. The messenger brought in three morning papers: there was nothing about Micklewright, but the *Globe* carried a front page picture of four attractive looking girls and Sir Jeremy Pilkington, Pilkington looking gay and very handsome. The caption read: *Sir J. Pilkington and Parisienne models in London for a Big River Mannequin Parade. See p. 7.* The other papers also carried the story. Tucked away in a corner was an account of the unsuccessful search by frogmen near Richmond. Gideon finished eating—and almost at once the telephone bell rang. He leaned across to take the call.

"Mr. Worby, sir, of Thames Division."

Worby, to commiserate.

"Put him through."

Worby's voice was pitched on a high note, without a hint of commiseration, and he announced without preamble:

"George, one of my chaps has had a brainwave."

"Good," said Gideon. "What kind?"

"He thinks that packet of industrial diamonds might have been stuck to the hull of a ship, and come off by accident."

Gideon said slowly: "Yes. Yes, it *is* a possibility, he's quite right." He thought: What's the matter with us, why didn't someone think of this before?"

"What I want to do is get the frogmen team busy," went on Worby. "They can cover a lot of the river if they start early—no searching needed, just a quick glance round the ships. We can say we're after a body, perhaps that Pierce child."

"Go ahead," Gideon agreed without hesitation.

"Right!"

"Which of your chaps was it?" Gideon wanted to know.

"You may remember him—the young one who was with you when you had your river trip."

"Addis, wasn't it?"

"Charlie Addis, that's the chap. Once he's on a job, he doesn't let go."

"He should make a good policeman," said Gideon. "Right."

"I'll get cracking," said Worby. " 'Bye—oh, *George*!"

"What is it?"

"Er—I—er—couldn't be sorrier about Micklewright."

"Nor could I," Gideon said drily.

"Have a problem with Van Hoorn now, won't you?" Worby asked.

"He's gone back to Holland for a few days, so that can keep," Gideon told him. "What about the River Parade?"

"Everything's set," said Worby. "Including the newspapers. Have they gone to town on this!"

"You'd expect them to go to town," Gideon remarked.

He rang off, and almost at once heard a movement in the next room. Was Hobbs in at last? He pondered young Addis's idea, recalled the eager, youthful face, then got up and went towards the door. It opened as he reached it, and he came face to face with Hobbs, who dropped back.

" 'Morning, Alec."

"Good morning," Hobbs said. He came inside as Gideon, in turn, backed away, his face finely drawn, obvious signs of anxiety in his eyes. "I haven't been down to *Information* or collected any reports yet," he said. "I've only just heard about Micklewright."

Gideon nodded, studying this man who came from such a different background and was dissimilar in so many ways, yet felt as deeply and as keenly for the reputation of the Force as any man who had been born and bred to it. He nodded again.

"Coffee?"

"No, thanks."

"Alec," Gideon said, "if I'm not careful the Micklewright case is going to become an obsession. It mustn't."

Hobbs gave a tight-lipped smile.

"Every newspaper, every television newsroom, the Home Secretary and our own Commissioner won't let us forget it. I had two newspapers on to me at my flat before I left.

"I daresay," Gideon weighed his words. "I don't mind how I feel or you feel or anyone else feels. This is a human problem. We've done our job, we've got to hand the papers over to the Legal Department to brief the Public Prosecutor. Except for preparing the details, it's out of our hands. I've got no comment to make and I want word to go out to every station—send a teletype message to all Divisions and sub-divisional stations, telling them to make none, and to warn all the men on their strength to say absolutely nothing."

"I should have realised you'd already decided what to do," Hobbs said.

"The real problem is to find someone quickly to replace Micklewright," went on Gideon. "Any ideas?"

Hobbs pondered.

"Do we want a man with a good knowledge of precious stones or someone with knowledge of smuggling up the river?"

"A river man," Gideon answered promptly. "Someone who knows the river and the different Forces concerned with policing it—he must know them well."

"I think I agree," Hobbs said. "There's only one man I can think of who answers to all that."

"Who?"

"Singleton of Thames Division," Hobbs said.

Gideon had been concentrating on possible successors to Micklewright among men at the Yard, and had not given a thought to anyone at the Division. He was surprised and, after the first few seconds, pleased that Hobbs should think of a man close to retiring age who might easily be allowed to wear out slowly. Singleton—Hobbs probably didn't know he was a friend of Micklewright. Gideon recalled all that had happened last night, remembered the challenge, the defiance, the gratitude.

"Alec, talk to Worby and put it to him this way. That you think Singleton would be the right man but until he, Worby, agrees, you don't want to put it up officially to me. You could even ask Worby to sound me out on it."

Hobbs's eyes crinkled at the corners as, for the first time that morning, he began to smile.

"I'll do just that."

"Make it your first job. Worby's in, he's already told me . . . " Gideon briefed Hobbs about what had happened, and Hobbs went back to his own room to talk to the Thames Division chief. Almost before he sat at his desk Gideon's telephone rang again.

"Yes."

"Mr. Hellier, sir, of EF Division," the operator said, and on that instance switched

Gideon's thoughts from diamonds and Micklewright to the missing Pierce child, of whom nothing had been heard for three days.

"Yes?" Gideon said.

"We know where the Pierce girl is," announced Hellier, without a word of preamble.

Chapter Seventeen

GERALDINE

Geraldine Pierce was still in the cave.

She was wide awake, but "Dick" was asleep.

She was dizzy with hunger for they had not eaten during the previous day. She had a dull headache and a sense of nausea.

She was secured by the strap and could not get at the buckle; she could move only a few inches. She felt cold, despite the touch of the man's body against her; her toes were freezing. She had a sense of hopelessness, brought on by hunger, pain, and utter helplessness. She *knew* what would happen if he caught her trying to get away again, she could still imagine the tightness of his hands round her throat.

There was nothing, now, that she could do.

Last night, late, as he had lain with her, she had pleaded and promised. If he would let her go she would tell no one, she would pretend she'd got lost or been on her own—

even run away. As she had pleaded she had seen the dull light in his eyes and had doubted whether he really heard what she said.

Afterwards, in that state of exhaustion she had become used to, she had said:

"You will let me go tomorrow, Dick, won't you?"

And he had said: "I'll never let you go. You're *mine*."

She had not uttered a word after that but had fallen asleep after a long time; and now she was awake, with the memory of his words and of his expression as he had uttered them. He had bared his teeth and spoken from deep in his throat.

"I'll never let you go. You're *mine*."

Now she began to think, drearily: "I can't get away. He means it, so I'll never get away."

Tears had flooded her eyes but she had repressed the impulse to cry for fear of waking him. After a while she began to toy with the idea of hitting him; if she could only be sure that he wouldn't wake she could wriggle and wriggle and get at the buckle beneath the bed.

How could she knock him out?

She stared at his weak face, the two days' old stubble, the slack mouth and eyelids smeared with white "sleep". There was nothing heavy or hard within hand's reach, so all she could use were her hands.

Hands.

His were very strong and he could kill her just by tightening them round her neck. Were *hers* strong enough? She moved them cautiously, to study them. They were quite long, dirty because she hadn't washed for several days, and her nails—

"*Geraldine! How often have I told you to file your nails!*"

Oh, Mummy, Mummy, Mummy!

She let her hands drop to the bed. They certainly weren't strong enough, and in any case she couldn't turn over and get them round his neck so as to grip tightly. It was hopeless, utterly hopeless, unless he were to go out and leave her. He had said something about going shopping today.

Even that was useless, though; he would tie her up so tightly she wouldn't have a chance. She hadn't any chance at all.

Unless—

She held her breath as an idea came into her mind. She saw his lower teeth and the top of his slack tongue as his head lolled forward awkwardly from the pillow. The *pillow*. She had seen a television picture only the other day—that age ago when she had run in and out of her home whenever she had wished. In the film, a woman had placed a pillow over a sleeping man's face and then pressed and pressed until his convulsive struggles had ceased.

The *pillow*.

She shifted round with infinite care so that she was facing him. She stretched her left arm over him and pulled the pillow a little further away from his head. He did not wake. She drew it free and his head fell just a little further forward. She could hardly breathe as she raised the pillow in one hand. Her mind was working very swiftly, and she could hear one of her school mistresses saying:

"*Think*, Geraldine, think before you *act*."

Think—

If she shifted her right arm high enough from the bed to touch part of the pillow beneath it, she could then hold it fast by lying on it. And she could stretch out her right arm and hold it tight on the other side. How long would it be before he stopped struggling? How long could *she* hold the pillow in position? Was she absolutely sure there was no other way?

She thought, no, no, there isn't.

She took a tighter hold on the pillow and eased her body up, drew the pillow across Dick's chest inch by inch, watching him tensely, frightened every moment that he would wake. If his eyes began to flicker that would be a sure sign.

She got the pillow beneath her body.

Her breathing was harsh and shallow and she was afraid that would disturb him. Now she had to decide whether to drop it on his face suddenly and put all her weight on to it, or whether to draw it gradually over his chin and then his face.

Gradually.

Gradually, gradually.

It was on a level with his chin, she steeled herself to make the final movement, when a dog barked close by.

On the instant, Dick woke.

He woke out of a sleep troubled by strange dreams of weird creatures and weird faces and staring eyes and beautiful bodies, to a loud yapping. He felt the pillow beneath his chin and knew immediately what Geraldine was trying to do. He flung himself backwards off the bed, snatched up the pillow and brought it down on to her head and face. He left it there and spun round towards the boarded-up window. The dog barked again and a boy called:

"Sprat, come here! Sprat."

The dog yapped again, less furiously. The boy called more gently:

"Leave it, Sprat, leave it."

At that moment, Jones made his great mistake; pushing back the bolt, he opened the door and peered out to find that some of the protecting sandstone had fallen. Across the stretch of water, only three or four yards away, the boy stood looking at him.

And as they stared at each other, Geraldine screamed:

"*Help me! Help me! Help me!*"

Jones jumped away from the door, saw Geraldine leaning on one elbow, her face suffused, her eyes screwed up, her mouth wide open; a series of high-pitched screams followed one another in quick succession. He sprang towards her and gripped the sheet, screwed up a corner and rammed it into her mouth so that her screams faded into a hoarse gurgling sound. Flinging the pillow over her face, he ran back to the door. He could hear no sound now, but saw the boy, fifty yards up the shallow side of the quarry, the dog at his heels. They were scrambling up, dirt and stones falling after them. Jones knew exactly where the path was, reached it and started after the boy, who saw him and made a wild effort to go faster. He drew level, only ten feet or so away from the boy, who would have had no chance but for the dog.

The dog leapt at Jones.

Jones kicked out, missed, and kicked again. The dog stumbled, steadied, and leapt at the man's hand. Its teeth buried themselves into the fleshy part of the ball of the thumb. Jones screamed in pain, lost his footing, and fell down several feet. The dog raced away; and a few seconds later both dog and boy reached the top of the quarry and disappeared. Jones came to rest nearer the foot of the path than the top, blood streaming from his hand, face scratched, knee suddenly painful where he had banged it on a stone. He picked himself up and staggered towards the mouth of the cave.

He went in.

He saw Geraldine, lying very still, the pillow on one side but the corner of the sheet still in her mouth.

He thought: she will tell the police what I have done.

He thought: I didn't hurt the boy, he doesn't matter. She mustn't tell anyone what I've done.

They'll put me away for ever if she tells them, he thought.

Her eyes were closed, and she did not seem to be breathing. He pulled the sheet slowly away from her mouth and dropped it. He picked up the pillow, held it in both hands, then lowered it slowly on to her face.

The boy was seen by a motorist, who stopped to see what was the matter.

The motorist drove furiously to the nearest house and telephoned the police.

The police were at the edge of the quarry in seven minutes and inside the cave in ten.

"We've found her, sir," Hellier said on the telephone to Gideon. "She's dead. Only been dead a few minutes, too."

"Have you tried—" Gideon began, helplessly.

"Tried the kiss—tried everything," Hellier said.

Gideon asked heavily: "Do the parents know?"

"I'm going to see them now," answered Hellier.

When he rang off he put the receiver down and sat at his desk for several minutes, with no comfort but his thoughts, and they were little enough. The girl *had* been in his manor. It was a well-hidden place but it should have been found. Whichever uniformed man covered the area would be in trouble for this, so would the detectives who had searched the quarry. In fact Hellier could not blame himself, but nevertheless he did. Not bitterly, but with a dull, aching sense of failed responsibility.

Now he had to go and tell the Pierces.

God knew how they would react.

And only yesterday Pierce had thrown up his job and joined in the hunt for his child. Poor devil. Poor, poor devil.

He sent for a car and was driven to the Pierces' home. No one had yet alerted the press, thank God, no one was outside the Pierces' house. It was after nine o'clock. Two school-children ran from a front door, hair and satchels flying, and a woman called from the open door:

"Mind you're careful in the High Street."

A bright-eyed, red-haired girl cried: "Okay, Mummy."

A smaller boy called: "'Course we will."

They raced past the police car without a glance at Hellier, but a woman opposite, brushing down a doorstep, stood up and stared across, then waved vigorously at someone out of Hellier's sight. He stepped out of the car and opened the iron gate of the Pierces' house, walked with long strides up to the front door, hesitated for a moment, then rat-tatted; the door seemed to shake. He waited, his face set, but there was no answer. He knocked again and pressed a bell-push at the side of the door. Then he glanced round. Faces were close to several windows and three women were now on the spot where the one had been. A car passed, the driver looking towards him.

The Pierces surely weren't out.

He knocked again and at last footsteps sounded on the stairs. A man's. Hellier drew himself up, massive, an almost forbidding figure. Pierce, with a red dressing-gown pulled but not tied about the waist, thin hair awry, face unshaved, peered at him.

Slowly, Pierce's expression changed. The tiredness drained away. The lines seemed to fade. A strange, defensive expression crept into his eyes, and Hellier knew that his mission had already been accomplished. Pierce realised why he had come. They stood absolutely still, and said nothing. Then Mrs. Pierce called from upstairs.

"Who is it?"

Pierce moistened his lips but didn't speak.

Hellier called, "It's me, Mrs. Pierce, Superintendent Hellier. I'm afraid I've—I've bad news for you."

Again there was silence; utter silence. Pierce moistened his lips again and moved back a step. Hellier did not know what to say or do. Pierce backed further away, and turned round; Hellier had an odd feeling that the man had forgotten he was present.

Wanda Pierce appeared at the head of the stairs.

"So she *is* dead." There was the flatness of resignation in her voice, a kind of fatalism, none of the hysteria which Hellier had expected.

"Stay there, Wanda," Pierce said in a level voice. "I'll come up to you." She ignored him and came down a step. "I said, stay there," he ordered.

"Superintendent, have you seen my daughter?" Wanda demanded.

"Yes," Hellier said.

"Is she—disfigured in any way?" asked Pierce.

"No," Hellier wanted to add: "Thank God," but he could not even put a warm or sympathetic inflection into his voice, he felt so taut.

"Where is she?"

"The—" he hesitated, boggled, over "mortuary" and said, "At the police station."

"In the mortuary?"

"Yes."

"My wife and I will want to see her. Please send a car for us in an hour's time," Pierce said.

He turned towards the foot of the stairs and then went up, slowly, to his wife. She hadn't moved again; she was all eyes in a pale, pale face. Hellier felt that they were oblivious of him, that he was utterly unimportant. He saw Mrs. Pierce's face pucker as her husband reached her, saw Pierce put an arm round her, had a strange sense that this weak little man had found a strength that he, Hellier, had not suspected him capable of possessing.

Mrs. Pierce began to cry.

Her husband led her out of sight, and a door closed. The sound of crying was shut off. Hellier closed his eyes and turned round slowly, as the woman from next door, Mrs. Edmond, came hurrying into the hallway.

For the first time, Hellier spoke in a relaxed and gentle voice.

"She's dead," he said. "But I think they'll be all right. I shouldn't go in yet, if I were you."

He did not hear Mrs. Edmond say in surprise to her neighbour: "He's got a heart after all."

Chapter Eighteen

"NEW" JOB

"Inspector! Mr. Worby wants you!"

Singleton looked up from the patrol boat into which he was stepping as a younger man came hurrying down the pier, kicked against one of the ridges and nearly fell.

"Pick 'em up, pick 'em up," growled Old Man River. "We don't want to have to fish *you* out." He strode up to the repair shop, past the stores, saw the store-keeper and young Addis sparring, pretended not to notice, and climbed the stone stairs to Worby's office. He tapped.

"Come on, come in." Worby was close to the door, just beneath the crossed cutlasses on the wall, souvenirs of the days when the River Police were armed with pistols, blunderbusses, knives and cutlasses. "'Morning, Jim," he went on, putting a book of regulations on a shelf. "What have you been up to?"

"What am I supposed to have done?"

Singleton struggled not to go on but lost the struggle. "Didn't upset the Commander last night, did I?"

Worby's half-grin faded.

"About Micklewright, you mean? Sad business that. Bloody sad. No. No, whatever you did certainly didn't upset him. Deputy Commander Hobbs put you up for a special mission and the Commander approved. So that leaves it up to me." The grin returned to the rather fleshy, almost sensuous face.

"Head messenger in chief?" asked Singleton, suspiciously.

"Replacement for Superintendent Micklewright on this industrial diamonds job, which means the Argyle-Morris murder, into the bargain," Worby said flatly.

At first Singleton did not take this in. Worby's works "Replacement for Superintendent Micklewright . . . " seemed to rebound off his mind. Then he thought: "The Warbler's ragging me."

"Come again."

"The Commander wants you to take over where Micklewright left off. He wants a man who knows the river, knows all the law enforcement groups who have a finger in river business, and who doesn't hate Dutchmen." Worby paused, as if he knew that the older man would need a few seconds to absorb what he was being told. "You'd have an office at the Yard, and the chaps who were working with Micklewright would be under you. And you'd keep your office here with all the usual facilities, and any two men you think would help most."

Singleton stared as if still not fully comprehending; and then he had a quick mind picture of his wife's face, and suddenly he beamed.

"I can't wait to tell Maggie," he said, in a near-falsetto voice. "I can't wait." Then he sobered, the weight of the responsibility of this assignment already making itself felt on his shoulders. "Thank you very much, sir." Worby liked to be appreciated.

"Don't thank me, Jim." The grin played about Worby's lips again. "If you think I can't run the station without you, you'll soon find out! Okay, then?"

"You bet it's okay!" Singleton's chest seemed to swell. "I'd like Tidy and Addis, please."

"They're yours."

"And Addis was telling me about this suction cap idea. You know what we want right away, don't you?"

"What?"

"The frogmen team." Already Singleton's excitement and exhilaration began to lose itself in the actual task; the planning. The policeman took over from the man almost at once. "They can operate in three pairs, leaving one in reserve. We can say they're looking for a body, people will believe that. All they have to do is swim round the barges and the lighters, anything tied alongside, and check if anything's stuck on. Right?"

Worby looked at him very straightly and without the vestige of a smile, and said:

"You're in charge, Jim."

Very slowly, Chief Inspector Singleton nodded. As slowly he said: "So I am."

Gideon felt as if he had been at the office all day, although it was only half-past eleven on that same morning.

The Micklewright affair had cut the Yard in two—one half saying in effect:

"Poor devil, shows coppers are human, too," the other half saying: "He's let the Force down." In their way both were right. With the Commissioner away and the Assistant Commissioner of the Criminal Investigation Department at a conference in South America, the brunt of it all fell on Gideon.

By ten o'clock, an Under Secretary at the Home Office had telephoned.

"The Home Secretary would like full details, Commander."

The Home Secretary would have to be satisfied with a brief précis of events.

By half-past ten, the senior public relations officer and the P.R.O. of the Home Office had been in his office.

"We want to make sure, Commander, that all our reports tally and that only the official statement is released to the press. Presumably you would like to approve the official statement."

"Yes," Gideon said. "Preferably in one sentence: the charge without comment."

"Commander, there will be a great deal of public interest . . ."

"Let's not make a meal out of it," Gideon said. "There may be a lot of ghouls about, but we don't have to feed them."

"What about the work Micklewright was doing?"

"Chief Inspector Singleton has taken over," Gideon said tersely.

After they had gone, the senior Press Officer of the Yard telephoned.

"I know you've problems, Commander, but so have we. Our telephones are ringing incessantly; we've been asked if a senior official will appear on a television programme tonight, and also on the radio. There will *have* to be a press conference during the day. And—" the P.O., an elderly man by Yard standards, changed his tone—"you're the best man for the job, George. Give 'em a show, let them bring the cameras in. You can handle them better than anyone here. If we refuse—" he paused, then went on into a silence which obviously worried him—"they'll put their own interpretation on it."

"Oh, all right, but it's to be a general conference, not specifically on Micklewright," Gideon conceded. "What time?"

"Is two o'clock all right?"

"Yes. Where?"

"The Lecture Hall," the Press Officer had answered.

Even when he had agreed to this, there was no rest from the case; it affected everyone he talked to, all the superintendents he briefed. But being Saturday, there was less briefing than usual, and no major crimes had been committed in the last twenty-four hours, so at least he could now concentrate on the two tasks which preoccupied him—the industrial diamonds investigation and the River Parade.

He spent some time pondering both, and just before twelve o'clock, rang for Hobbs.

"Going to Lord's this afternoon?" he asked, as the door opened and Hobbs appeared.

"No," Hobbs answered. "I've asked Worby to take me up and down the river."

"Sit down." Gideon leaned back in his chair. "Seen any fresh angle yet?"

"No," said Hobbs, "I still think the helicopter idea is the most likely way they'd raid the boat, but the more I think of it the less probable it seems. I've been through the whole file—had Prescott here most of the morning. He's absolutely satisfied that the protection from the Embankment is foolproof. Securial are co-operating, so is Pilkington."

"Probably pass off without any trouble at all," mused Gideon. "Has Prescott noticed anything at all unusual?"

"No," answered Hobbs. "He's briefed all his men on all the shifts: if there's anything even slightly suspicious or unusual, they're to report. I'll check with Worby from the river—are *you* going to Lord's?"

"After this press conference, I thought I'd look in on Prescott."

Hobbs gave an unexpectedly free smile.

"Don't know that it will get you anywhere," he told Gideon. "*He's* going to Lord's!" Prescott was probably the most enthusiastic cricket fan on the Force. "Shall I warn him you may look in?" he added.

"Don't think I would," said Gideon slowly. "Anyhow," he went on, "I may be so bad tempered after this press conference that I won't go near the place. That reminds me." He reached for the telephone, but almost at the same moment it rang. He lifted the receiver. "Yes? . . .

Yes, put him through. *Worby*," he added in an aside to Hobbs. "Hello, Warbler . . . Yes . . . Good . . . Tell him to come and see me at three o'clock . . . Yes, I'll be here."

He rang off.

"Singleton's got the frogmen out already, the Warbler says he's mustard keen." He smiled, rather dourly. "He'd like to report to one of us this afternoon."

"Someone must have told him about the briefing sessions." Hobbs said, and almost before his last word faded, the telephone rang again. But the two men were used to the almost non-stop sequence of events, and it seldom ruffled them.

"Your wife is on the line, sir . . . "

"Hello, Kate, what time were you thinking of coming back? . . . That's good, I'll be late . . . We'll go out somewhere tonight, and let the kids look after themselves . . . 'Bout six, then. Goodbye, dear."

Hobbs was already at the door.

The Chief Press Officer was a tall, droll-faced man, with rubbery lips and a pointed chin, a thin neck and a prominent Adam's apple which he tried to hide by wearing a high collar a little too large for him. He came into Gideon's office just before two o'clock. Gideon had had a sandwich and beer lunch, and was at the window.

"All ready, sir?" said the C.P.O.

"How long do you think they'll want?" asked Gideon.

"Thirty or forty minutes, sir. Both television channels have sent a camera team. Er—I've briefed a couple of the Agencies and they'll lead in with easy ones."

As he went along to the Lecture Hall, where special briefings were often held, Gideon pulled down his jacket and ran his hand over his wiry hair. Two uniformed men were outside the hall and opened the door. A babble of talk sounded and the room was full of smoke. Someone called out: "The Commander," and there was an immediate hush. Most of the men got to their feet; so did the only two women present. Gideon went to the front of the room where a table with a notepad, glasses and a carafe of water stood beside various microphones, marked B.B.C., B.B.C.1, B.B.C.2, A.T.V., Granada and several others. A small man tapped one of these and there was a curious kind of sound from the back of the room; so this was the public address microphone, thought Gideon. Two television cameramen and several other photographers were in the front row.

The C.P.O. cleared his throat. "Gentlemen—*ladies* and gentlemen, I beg your pardon—Commander Gideon has been able to allocate you thirty minutes. The shorter your questions, the more he can answer."

"Commander," a man asked promptly, "do you think that over half a million pounds' worth of precious stones should be shown on so vulnerable a place as the river?"

Gideon pursed his lips.

"Ask the Thames Division that and they'll tell you that the Thames is the least vulnerable place in London. They lose very little from the docks and wharves. As for the question—it's up to the people who own the jewels."

"Do you disapprove or approve, Commander?"

"I would complain if they took unnecessary risks, but they don't appear to be taking any."

"Were you allowed enough time to prepare?" asked another man.

"It isn't time we need, it's more staff," Gideon countered. "We can't police London as well as we'd like to, because we are fifteen or twenty per cent below strength."

"Damned good point," murmured the C.P.O. Pencils sped over note books of all shapes and sizes.

"Are you satisfied with the security precautions for the River Parade, sir?" A man called from the back of the hall.

"Yes."

One of the women asked in a quiet voice:

"Do you think that special displays of this kind *should* be allowed to draw off police protection from other parts of London?"

"No. And it isn't doing so."

"Surely it *must*, Commander." She looked a little mouse of a woman, but she was persistent.

"All it does do is to cause a lot of policemen's wives to grumble because their husbands have to work overtime," Gideon answered, and won a little laughter.

"Do they get paid for overtime,

Commander?" asked the other woman.

"They either get paid or they get time off when things are slack."

"Are things *ever* slack?" That was an American voice from the side of the hall.

There was a general, louder laugh.

"Sometimes even our bad men behave themselves," Gideon remarked, and the laughter was redoubled. Gideon suddenly realised that he was enjoying himself, but he checked his tendency to encourage light-heartedness.

Into the tail-end of the laughter, a man with a Scottish accent asked: "Were you satisfied with the way the search for Geraldine Pierce was carried out, Commander?"

The mood of the conference changed almost visibly. Smiles were wiped off every face, men sat up more erectly, Gideon, aware of the danger of relaxing as he had relaxed, gave himself a moment or two to think what best to say.

"I was satisfied with the way it was carried out, yes. Obviously I wasn't satisfied with the results."

"Shouldn't the hiding-place have been found earlier?"

"It's easy to be wise after the event." Gideon pointed to a map on the wall behind him, on which each division was shown in a pastel shade of contrasting colour, the river winding in dark blue through the centre. "Constable," he called one of the uniformed policemen, "come and outline the area which was searched, will you?"

As he spoke, he thought: "My God, I hope he *knows* the area." But his fears faded as the policeman approached the map without a moment's hesitation and eased the tension by drawing out a truncheon to use as a pointer. "That stretch of river is seven miles long," Gideon said. "Along much of it there is scrub and bush. There are hundreds of small boats, boat sheds, boat-houses, caravans and abandoned motor-cars, and in the summer several official and some private camping sites. Every single place had to be searched . . . Point to Richmond Park, Constable—thank you. That is a Royal Park, open to the public by day, closed by night to motor traffic. Its area is . . . Now Ham Common, Constable."

Gideon described the different sections

of the area quietly and precisely, and at last he finished.

"The search took three days. To comb the area thoroughly needed twice or three times as many men working for at least a week. It was organised down to the last detail, and I don't know of anything else that could have been done."

There was a long silence; and then, quite spontaneously, a little outburst of applause. Again Gideon felt a sense of satisfaction; and again, there was an immediate and sobering change of subject.

"Commander, do you think the arrest and charging of a senior official of the police will do harm to the public image of the police?"

Slowly, Gideon answered: "I don't know whether it will. I know that it shouldn't."

"Do you know Superintendent Mickle-wright well, Commander?"

"Yes. Very well."

"Are you aware that there are rumours that he was drinking too much?"

"Yes. I am aware that there are all kinds of rumours—including one that he took a sedative and had a drink afterwards."

"Commander," said a small man with a curiously lop-sided face, "do you think that a man in Superintendent Micklewright's distraught and distressed state of mind should have been assigned to an investigation of international importance? Wasn't he *bound* to upset the Dutch police?"

That question, with the sting in its tail, was almost deadly in its impact, and Gideon felt every eye turn towards him, knew that everyone was hanging on to his words.

Chapter Nineteen

A REPORT IN THE AFTERNOON

Gideon's first thought was, I shouldn't have laid myself open to this. His second, I must be very careful indeed. His third, I mustn't hesitate too long. It did not occur to him to take the easy way out, the way which would no doubt be approved by the Home Secretary and his superiors at the Yard, and to say simply: "No comment."

He looked squarely at the sea of faces confronting him. "Failure can be frustrating and upsetting," he said slowly. "The loss of industrial diamonds has been a harassment to the Western European police for some time. Only recently was there reason to suspect that some of the diamonds might be sent to England. We work closely with all the European police forces, sometimes in direct contact, sometimes through Interpol. In every case of joint investigation we assign the man whom we think most familiar with the kind of crime being investigated.

"Superintendent Micklewright is a world authority," he added. "He has been asked to advise on similar cases in South Africa, South America and the United States. He made—and helped to make—sufficient progress with the case for us to follow a different line of investigation—along the whole course of the river. At no time did he give any indication that he was not competent to carry out his duties. On the contrary, he carried them out well. Chief Inspector Singleton is now in charge of that particular line of inquiry and of the investigation." He paused, looked round, saw the man with the lop-sided face start to speak, and went on in a tone of absolute finality: "I have nothing more to say on that subject, gentlemen."

Two would-be questioners sat down, without protest.

Gideon was asked a few more questions which he answered briefly, posed for half a dozen photographs, and then went out surrounded by a group of newspaper men. The constable who had used his truncheon as a pointer was at the door.

"Thanks, Constable," Gideon said.

"Pleasure, sir."

Gideon walked on, turned a corner and went back to his office with a chorus of "Thanks," "Goodbyes," and "See yous," following him. The Chief Press Officer was at his elbow.

"Don't want to sound pompous, Commander, but that was a bloody good show."

Gideon stared out of the window and went over the river, bright in the afternoon sun.

"I hope so," he said. "We'll see what they make of it tomorrow."

"You won them over completely, sir."

Gideon turned to look at him.

"That's the trouble," he said, soberly. "They shouldn't have to *be* won over. They ought to be on our side all the time."

"There isn't one who won't make the point about us being under-established," the other man prophesied. "Er—is there anything I can get you?"

"No," Gideon said. "Chief Inspector Singleton is due at three o'clock. Try to make sure he's not button-holed by the press, will you?"

"They wouldn't get any change out of Old Man River," the C.P.O. said confidently.

It was ten minutes to three before Gideon was on his own. No new reports were on his desk, and none on Hobbs's, but at half a minute to three there were footsteps in the passage, followed by an over-loud knock at the door. This would be Singleton.

"Come in!" Gideon called.

Singleton looked a different man from the grim and defiant one whom Gideon had seen last night. Then he had had to brace himself to make an effort: now he had an almost buoyant confidence, and looked years younger.

"Sit down, Chief Inspector," Gideon said. "And while I think of it, your man Addis had a bright idea, didn't he?"

"*Very* bright ,sir." Singleton beamed. "The frogmen found three more packets, too."

With great deliberation he opened his black brief-case and took out three waterproof packets which had been found. These he placed, very precisely, on Gideon's desk, glancing up at Gideon each time he withdrew his hand.

Gideon stared at the packets, fascinated; it was so improbable that he could hardly believe his eyes. All thought of the press conference, the awkward questions, sudden depression, vanished. He met Singleton's gaze, and for a few seconds, noticed nothing. Then he saw the hint of triumph in them, and realised how elated the Thames Division man must be.

He drew a deep breath.

"It's a long time since I've been excited," he remarked.

Singleton gave an explosive little laugh. "Me, too!"

"Addis didn't plant 'em there, I suppose," Gideon said.

"You could ask him, sir. He's in the room which Mr. Hobbs put at our disposal."

"I'll take your word for it," said Gideon. "Where were they found?"

"One on a barge opposite the Millwall Docks,—the old section, sir. One on a lighter moored up river with eight barges in tow. And one on a Dutch coaster which came in with some chocolate and cocoa."

Gideon picked up one of the packets, weighted it in his hand, then tossed it back to Singleton.

"Better make sure it *does* contain diamonds."

Singleton nodded, and, with very great care, slit one edge of the waterproof covering. Inside was a polythene bag. Singleton slit this with the same finicky care and took out a fold of linen. As before, the linen was lined with wash-leather, from which, kept in place by a strip of transparent plastic, innumerable diamond chips scintillated in all directions like tiny grains of sand.

All three packets contained the same weight of diamonds; each packet was worth about two thousand pounds on the commerical market. There was now no longer any doubt that Van Hoorn was right in believing that a substantial quantity of the stolen Dutch diamonds were being brought to London.

"Any ideas?" Gideon asked Singleton, after a long pause.

"May I report to date, sir?"

That was evasive, but no doubt Singleton had his reasons.

"Yes," said Gideon.

"There wasn't any doubt that Screw Smith and a man not yet known to us took Argyle-Morris away from his flat. Captain Kenway was right about that. One of the P.L.A. gate policemen saw them go into the No. 2 Gate of the West India Docks and says he saw them leave about two hours later. He's not positive the same men were in it but he was sure the same car went out—a black Ford Anglia. And Screw Smith owns a Ford Anglia."

Gideon nodded.

"Argyle-Morris's body was found at a place we call Dead Man's Rest—sometimes bodies come up there when the river's a bit lower than usual. There's a current that swings them out of midstream on to a point off the Isle of Dogs. Every time we've taken a corpse out of there we've discovered that the victim fell in somewhere between Wapping and Limehouse. That's a simple fact, sir."

"Yes. Go on."

"A Vauxhall Victor was seen along by Wapping High Street at half-past eleven the night before the body was found. It stopped for about three minutes. It was seen by a night watchman at a tea warehouse in the High Street—less than half a mile from our station, sir. We can't trace the Vauxhall Victor, but we're after it. And we *do* know that Screw Smith has been seen in a V.V. two or three times lately with a man unknown to the Divisional Police."

Gideon said:

"Superintendent Roswell is giving you plenty of help, then."

"As he did Mr. Micklewright, sir."

"Good."

"We could pick up Smith," Singleton hazarded, "and we might get something out of him, but I've just finished reading Mr. Micklewright's report, as far as he'd written it."

Gideon waited.

"It's obvious that he was coming round to the Dutch view that this diamond racket is pretty big," Singleton went on, "and now we've found this little lot—" he motioned to the three packets—"it looks more likely than ever. It stands to reason that these packets come up from the estuary by night, a frogman goes over and fastens them on to the hulls with a magnet, actually, not a suction cup, and *another* frogman goes out later to pick them up. One of these packets has enough slime on it to show that it's been on the same spot for days, if not weeks. There's no telling how often packets are brought over, or how many there are in all, but apparently it's been going on for a long time, *and*—" Singleton hesitated, as if for the first time he began to wonder whether he was taking Gideon along with him—"it's very big business, sir."

Gideon nodded, and echoed: "Very."

"And Smith isn't big business, any more than Dave Carter was. We could pick him up, we might even prove a case against him, but in doing so we risk losing bigger game."

Gideon nodded again. "So?" he asked, with raised brows.

"I'd leave him, sir, and I'd put these packets back—empty—and watch the vessels we took 'em from," advised Singleton. "That might lead us to the big fish." He grinned suddenly, partly from tension, partly because of his native sense of humour. "Wouldn't like Van Hoorn to know what we'd done, though."

"No," said Gideon thoughtfully.

"Think it would work, sir?" Singleton looked anxious.

"I think it might. When would you put the packets back?"

"Tonight, sir," answered Singleton. "I've got the frogmen standing by in case that's what you decide."

Gideon hid a smile, and hesitated for a few moments before replying. He was attracted by the idea, and it certainly might work. He would have told Singleton to go ahead straight away, but for the murder of Argyle-Morris and the fact that Screw Smith might get away with that if the trail were allowed to go cold. The decision had to be made on a basis of what would give the best chance of catching Argyle-Morris's murderer.

"What about the girl—named Mary Rose, isn't she?"

"As a matter of fact—" Singleton sounded almost glib—"Addis reports that she's been going around in a Vauxhall Victor lately."

"With a driver not yet known to us, I take it," Gideon said drily.

"That's right, sir."

"What about the man who started all this? Carter."

"He's up for a second hearing on Wednesday—we should have a good idea of whether he plays any part in the smuggling by then," Singleton answered. "Roswell—Mr. Roswell—isn't sure he can make the attempted murder charge stick, as the girl's evidence won't be too reliable now." Singleton was obviously making a considerable effort not to plead for his way, but the effort was putting a great strain on him.

Gideon said abruptly: "All right, we'll give it a go. But keep tails on Screw Smith and ferret out everything you can about him as if you were going to charge him with murder."

"I won't lose him, sir." Singleton said confidently. "He's a very nasty piece of work."

Half an hour later as Gideon was driving along the Embankment, undecided whether or not to call in at the Divisional Headquarters, he remembered Addis, at the Yard; he should have looked in to see him. Pity. It was a remarkable development, and the more he pondered it the more likely it seemed that the river was being used for crime organised on a big scale. Anyone who planned this industrial diamond job and could both afford and be willing to leave a cache of diamonds hidden for several months, must surely be a master criminal.

There *was* a carefully planned series of crimes on the river with regard to the industrial diamonds.

There might also be a skilfully planned "once only" raid on the River Parade diamonds. Any man bold and daring enough to organise the one might well be bold and daring enough to organise the other.

He shrugged the thought aside as fanciful, but it made him decide to go into the Divisional Headquarters. The Chief Inspector in charge was a youthful, blond man also named Smith, obviously anxious to make a good impression, as obviously determined not to let his superior down.

"Mr. Prescott's taken a few hours off, sir, but he'll look in later. Meanwhile one thing has cropped up. May be nothing in it, of course, but Mr. Prescott wanted to know everything that was unusual."

"So do I," said Gideon.

"It's a report from P.C. Toller, who signed on half an hour ago," Smith reported. "He's on duty at the pier head, we always have at least one man on duty at the *Belle Casino*. Last night he saw Mr. St. John—Sir Jeremy Pilkington's second-in-command, sir—go from the *River Belle* to the *Belle Casino*, and stay only for about ten minutes."

"Is that unusual?" Gideon asked.

"Usually St. John stays longer. The peculiar thing about last night, though, was that a man followed St. John to the pier head in a Mini-Minor. There was a girl in the car with him, and P.C. Toller says he recognised the girl."

"Oh," said Gideon. "Who was she?"

"A Mary Rose Shamley, the girl friend of that poor devil pulled out of the river a couple of days ago," Smith answered.

"I want to see Toller at once," Gideon decided on the instant. "If he isn't on the station, get him. And I want to talk to Mr. Singleton, at the Yard. After that to Mr. Hobbs, who's with a Thames Division patrol somewhere between here and Greenwich. Hurry!"

Chapter Twenty

GIDEON'S SPEED

"Singleton."

"Yes, sir."

"I want an Identi-kit picture of the unidentified man who's driven that Vauxhall Victor with the Mary Rose girl."

"Yes, sir."

"And I want you or Addis or anyone who's seen the girl out here at Division with the picture—*soon*."

"It will be Addis, sir."

"Ring me back when it's all in hand."

"Yes, sir."

Gideon rang off—and the telephone rang again.

"Mr. Hobbs, sir."

"Alec, this is *very* urgent. St. John's had some heavy gambling debts and paid four hundred and fifty pounds off last night on the *Belle Casino*. I've talked to the manager. He paid off a thousand ten days ago. And he was followed by a man who may be an associate of Screw Smith. Got that?"

Hobbs said: "Clearly."

"I want you to see Pilkington, tell him—in fact have a confrontation with Pilkington, see if he can get anything out of St. John."

"He could, too."

"Where are you now?"

"Near Waterloo Pier."

"I've told Pilkington we're sending someone to see him, he'll be there at half-past five," said Gideon.

"So will I."

"I'll be here or at home," Gideon rang off, then paused for the first time since he had heard about St. John being followed. Chief Inspector Smith, a little apprehensive and greatly impressed, saw the quality he had heard about in Gideon but never seen—this tremendous power of concentration. Gideon was also aware of it. From time to time an event acted on him like a powerful stimulant; he could think, reason, make decisions and move three times as fast as usual.

Now he was thinking . . .

Frogmen, underwater specialists, who was there in London? He spoke sharply. "Smith!"

"Sir."

"Get Colonel Abbotson of the Royal Marines. He's stationed at Greenwich. Find out where he lives, where he is now, get him for me."

"By telephone, sir?"

"Yes."

Smith turned and almost ran out of the office. Gideon pushed back his chair and breathed more freely. He could safely relax, for there was nothing more he could do himself at the moment. He felt very dry-mouthed and suddenly longed for a cup of tea. "Anyone outside?" he called.

A man answered: "Sergeant Mee, sir," and a stout, middle-aged policeman appeared.

"Tell someone to send me some tea, in a pot, hot and strong."

"Right away, sir."

Gideon put his hand to his pocket and smoothed the bowl of a big pipe. He had not smoked it for years, all he ever smoked these days were cigars, but at times of stress he found himself doing this; there was something companionable about the briar. If Lemaitre were here he could think aloud. "Lem," he would say, "I've seen a possibility that scares the living daylights out of me." Lemaitre would ask him what and he would hedge. Funny, how one got used to the companionship of certain men, and how one missed it. Would Hobbs ever be that sort of companion? It wasn't likely. They came from different backgrounds, looked at things from different angles.

He was half-way through his second cup of tea when Singleton called:

"We've done better than an Identi-kit picture, sir."

"What have you got?"

"A photograph—very good likeness, too. I'm having copies run off. We can have twenty or thirty at once."

Thank God for a man of quick intelligence!

"Send some over," Gideon ordered, "and get plenty done. Have those waterproof packets been replaced yet?"

"No, sir."

"Get 'em back—fast." Gideon was about to ring off when he had a moment of compunction—it was unfair to let Singleton work in a fog. "It's possible those packets were stuck where they were as a precaution. There could be a daily inspection to check whether we've found them. It that's the case they'll know we have."

"Good God!" exclaimed Singleton. "I hadn't thought of that."

"And today I don't want anyone scared off," Gideon said. "There could be a connection between your job and the River Parade—and keep that right under your hat, even from your assistants."

Singleton said faintly: "They wouldn't believe me, sir."

Gideon almost laughed.

It was a quarter to six when Addis brought the photographs. By Gideon's standards he was young, but he was standing up to success and excitement very well, watched his words and his manner carefully, and was as neat as the reefer jacket of the Thames Division could allow. His white collar and tie almost glistened.

P.C. Toller, who had noticed St. John and put in the report, identified the man and the girl instantly.

"I'm *quite* sure they were in the Mini, sir, and just as sure the driver was the same man who drove the Vauxhall. The lighting's especially good just there—the Superintendent had it improved in case anyone tried to raid the Casino."

Good for Prescott; very good for Toller. Toller went out and Gideon turned to Addis, who was pinning a photograph of the unidentified driver of the Vauxhall Victor, side by side with Argyle-Morris's girl, on to a notice board.

"Who took the photograph, Addis?"

"I did, sir."

"For any special reason?"

"Er—in a way, sir," Addis said, a little hesitantly.

"Go on."

"I don't think we—the Force—use photography enough, sir. I've always thought that we could have a small camera—concealed miniature would do, sir—as part of our equipment. It would facilitate identification and often be invaluable in court, sir." Obviously Addis wondered whether he had been overbold, and was very formal.

"Worth thinking about," Gideon conceded. "Have you talked about this to Superintendent Worby?"

"Er—no, sir. He's above my—" Addis broke off and gave a broad, embarrassed grin. "I've mentioned it to Mr. Singleton, though."

"Have Mr. Singleton mention it to Superintendent Worby," Gideon said drily. As he spoke the telephone bell rang and he nodded dismissal to Addis and picked up the instrument. "Yes?"

"There's a message from Mr. Hobbs, sir."

"What is it?"

"He says that both men are available and he's going in to see them right away."

"Thanks," grunted Gideon, and as he rang off, he knew that he had never wanted to be anywhere more than he wanted to be with Hobbs right now.

St. John found nothing surprising in the summons to Pilkington's flat overlooking Kensington Gardens; in fact he had rather expected it and had kept himself in readiness. He lived alone, and left his flat at half-past five. He did not notice that as he took the wheel of his Jaguar a Mini Minor turned out of a row of parked cars, following him so skilfully that the driver of the car saw him go into the building where Pilkington lived.

Nor did he, or his shadows, realise that the police had both cars under constant surveillance, and their progress was being reported to *Information*.

Pilkington was alone.

"Hello, Hugh," he said, as he sprawled on a big couch, a little over-dressed, a little too flamboyant. "One or two things I want to talk about, dear boy." St. John's lips almost curled, he was so sickened by this man's foppishness; he and Gentian would make a good pair, he thought. Yet the 'one or two' things all proved pertinent, and no one could doubt Pilkington's intelligence.

Ten minutes after he had arrived, Hobbs came in. That was the first jolt to St. John's complacence, but he quickly reminded himself that these men were old friends. The second jolt to his complacence came with a change in Pilkington's voice; a hardening.

"Hugh, I've been hearing things about you I don't like," he said.

"You should hear what I hear about you,"

St. John retorted, masking a rising consternation.

"You've never heard that I've taken bribes to sell anyone out," Pilkington replied.

St. John was so shocked that he could only stand and gape; then he turned and glared at Hobbs. He was breathing very hard.

"I've never taken a bribe in my life! If your bloody flat-foots—"

"That's a bit insolent, Hugh."

"Insolent be damned. If the police—"

"The police would like to know where you obtained the four hundred and fifty pounds with which you paid off your gambling debts last night," Hobbs said quietly, "and where you obtained the thousand pounds you paid off a week ago." He held out a photograph of the girl and of the driver of both the Mini Minor and the Vauxhall Victor. "How well do you know these people, Mr. St. John?"

St. John stared, then said tartly:

"I've never seen them before."

"The man followed you here this afternoon and is parked in Kensington Road at this moment," Hobbs stated.

St. John caught his breath.

"He can't be!"

"Don't be a bloody fool, old boy," Pilkington advised in a mild voice. "He's there. Saw him myself when I looked out of the window. What's on? We want to know."

"Nothing's on, I tell you!"

"Mr. St. John," Hobbs said, "you still have time to undo any harm you've done."

"I haven't committed any crime," St. John said harshly.

Pilkington stood up, and very slowly moved towards him.

"Hugh," he said, "if I have to I'll squeeze the truth out of you." He had strong-looking hands. "But Hobbs is right, you've time to make amends. And you may not have committed any crime—*yet*. But if there's any trouble on the *River Belle* and you're party to it—"

Hobbs interrupted him. "This man—" he tapped the photograph—"is wanted for questioning in connection with a particularly brutal murder."

St. John paled. "I don't know anything about a murder," he rasped.

"What have you been up to, Hugh?" insisted Pilkington. He placed his hands on the top of St. John's arms. "Let's have it, old chap."

St. John began to sweat.

"I think it will save time if you come with me to Scotland Yard," Hobbs said in sudden impatience. "I'll keep you informed, Jeremy."

"No," St. John said, catching his breath. "There's no need for that, I—I—" he drew himself up—"I've been selling information, but I don't know who to, or what they're planning to do." He wiped the sweat off his forehead. "At first I thought someone wanted to sabatoge the Parade, but . . ."

He began to talk so freely that it seemed he was almost glad to get the burden off his mind.

"Go back to your flat, stay in all the evening, telephone Sir Jeremy if you are approached at all—just ask some question about the Parade," Hobbs ordered. "Take no notice if you're followed. If you do telephone, we shall be told at once and we will get in touch with you. Is that clear?"

St. John nodded, mutely.

From the door he looked back unbelievingly at the man for whom he had had such little respect.

It was a quarter to seven when the telephone in Smith's office rang and the operator said: "Colonel Abbotson, sir."

"Put him through—and then telephone my wife and tell her I'll be later than I expected and may not get home until midnight," Gideon said.

"Yes, sir. Colonel Abbotson on the line now, sir."

Gideon tightened his grip on the receiver. "Colonel Abbotson?"

"Yes, Commander."

"I'm sorry to worry you, but I think you're the one man most likely to help in a problem we have on our hands," Gideon told him. "Where are you at the moment?"

"I've just come back from an afternoon of golf."

"Can we dine together?" asked Gideon.

"Delighted." Abbotson did not even pause. "Shall we say eight o'clock? And if you'll come here it will help—the R.M. Club?"

"Thank you, I'd like that," Gideon said.

As he rang off, reflecting on the pleasure it was to deal with men who wasted no time, Hobbs came in. Gideon did not need telling that Hobbs was fully satisfied with the way things had gone. He nodded slightly, and his lips curved in a faint, tight-lipped smile.

"We've got St. John, anyhow," he said. "He was taking bribes. We can't place the two men he dealt with, but he's given us a good description of each. Apparently they met in an apartment which is let furnished to a man named Brown—but this was obviously a blind."

"No photographs?" Gideon asked, and then went on hurriedly: "Does he know what's planned?"

"Only that they're after the diamonds and wanted details and dimensions of the *River Belle*."

Gideon rubbed his chin.

"I wonder why." He paused for a moment, then asked: "Anything more to to tonight, Alec?"

"Not unless you can think of something."

"I can," Gideon said. "You can square my conscience. Take Kate out to dinner. I'm going to . . ." He explained a little, watching Hobbs, seeing what he thought was a glint of pleasure in his eyes.

"I'll be happy to," Hobbs said, and a smile curved his lips again. "Can I know why you're dining with a Colonel of the Royal Marines?"

"Yes," said Gideon. "Three or four years ago a Naval launch went down near London Bridge and there were some dangerous explosives on board as well as some secret apparatus. Abbotson was in charge of the salvage job, and it was quite a job."

"It was a midget submarine, wasn't it?" asked Hobbs, and on the instant his expression changed. "Good God!" he exclaimed. "Attack from *beneath* the water! Is that what's in your mind?"

"Yes," said Gideon slowly. "That's exactly what's in my mind."

Chapter Twenty-one

THE RIVER PARADE

Colonel Abbotson looked about forty, was fresh-faced and keen-eyed, with close-cropped fair hair and a close clipped fair moustache. He had a well-scrubbed look about him. He was standing in the hall of the small club, exclusive, Gideon knew, to holders of decorations for valour in both war and peace. It was an old Georgian house not far from Berkeley Square and might still have been a private home. The carved staircase was luxuriously carpeted, oil portraits of men with distinguished and often slightly mysterious war records were on the walls. There was ample room in the panelled dining-room, and Abbotson had selected a table in an alcove which was exactly right for a *tête-à-tête*.

"I imagined you would want to keep this quiet," he said.

"Couldn't be more right," said Gideon, "and I couldn't be more grateful for your help."

"Haven't got it yet," Abbotson said with a smile. He paused as a waiter appeared at his shoulder. "I can recommend the smoked salmon—the roast duck's pretty good here, too, if you care for duck— Good, I'll have the same. And a Montrachet, I think, or do you prefer something more robust?"

Soon, they were free to talk.

Gideon outlined the situation as it was, and then asked earnestly:

"What I want to know is, could small one- or two-man submarines come up the Thames from the estuary, or from a wharf or warehouse, plant these packets, or take 'em away, without being detected?"

Abbotson answered promptly. "Unless we were looking for them, they probably wouldn't be detected. Expecting a modern Van Tromp, are you?"

"And are there small vessels which a man—a frogman—can get in and out of, under water, without being seen?"

"Yes. Frogmen in certain branches are trained to it," said Abbotson. He paused again as the waiter returned with two plates of smoked salmon and a third plate of finely cut brown bread and butter.

"I've been recalling all I can about this River Parade," he continued as the waiter disappeared. "There will be four or five hundred people on board, won't there?"

"Yes. And a safe full of diamonds and other jewels," Gideon told him. "What I'm wondering is whether one of these submarines could come close enough to fasten a limpet mine on to the bottom of the *River Belle*, hover in safety until the mine went off, then move in during the pandemonium which would follow, get the safe, and take it away. Once it was in the water the weight of the safe wouldn't be quite so important, would it?" When Abbotson didn't answer at once, he went on a little self-consciously. "I know it sounds melodramatic, but—"

"It sounds damned feasible," Abbotson said firmly. "If the crooks were indifferent to drowning a few dozen or so of the people in the ship it would be perfectly practicable. The people on the bridges and banks would be helpless, of course. In fact we *did* something like it on an exercise off the Isle of Wight a few months ago."

"Did it work?"

"Like a charm."

Gideon began to feel very much better, and he picked up his knife and fork and began to eat. He was aware of the delicate flavour of the salmon yet ate without concentrating on what he was doing. Abbotson helped himself to a piece of bread and butter.

"And you want us to watch the river on Monday evening. Is that right?"

"Yes," said Gideon, simply.

"You'll have to pull some strings, and it's the week-end," Abbotson said. "I'd guess your safest way would be to get the Home Secretary to talk to the Minister of Defence. I could get everything ready for an exercise in the estuary," he went on. "We've a team at Shoeburyness, no need to worry on that score. We just want the word 'go'."

"It is a difficult time," said the Permanent Under Secretary at the Home Office, "but if you think it essential, Commander—"

"I do," said Gideon, uncompromisingly.

"Very well, Mr. Gideon, I will talk to my colleagues," promised the Home Secretary.

"Thank you very much, sir."

"If we've the men and equipment available, I don't see why not," said the Minister of Defence. "I imagine it will be a waste of time but it will give the Royal Marines an opportunity to exercise this particular team of under-water experts. I will see whether I can find the Commander-General."

It was half-past four on the Sunday afternoon when the telephone woke Gideon out of a nap he had been quite sure he would never have. The sound of piano music came softly from the front room, as did Kate's humming. She often went there with the girls, and persuaded Penelope to play her favourite tunes.

Gideon got up and went to the telephone.

Colonel Abbotson said jubilantly: "It's on, Commander!"

Gideon forgot the fact that he was drowsy, forgot everything but the almost sickening excitement at what might happen. He could not tell Kate. He could not tell anybody. He could only warn Thames Division and the land divisions to stand by, and most of them expected an attack, if one came at all, from the Embankment, from one of the other ships, or from the air.

Only Hobbs knew.

Singleton was at Waterloo Pier, in touch by radio-telephone with Abbotson, believing that this precaution was against the possibility of a major robbery and an attempted getaway by water. He did not think it very likely but he was in no mood to be critical of Gideon. Addis and Tidy were in a patrol boat with another coxswain, also in contact by radio-telephone.

All that Monday the final arrangements were made on the *River Belle*. Gentian and his girls were in a last minute panic to get the final drapes up in time. The boat was being decorated with flowers, quite exquisite in their beauty. The electricians were putting the finishing touches to the lighting. The models were rehearsing in one of the big stores. The police and the Securial guards were having a rehearsal to make sure that all the precautions for the jewels were foolproof.

Kate, Gideon and Penelope were dressing for the great occasion, Penny with an excitement due at least partly to the fact that her escort was to be Deputy Commander Hobbs, Kate with a little disquiet, for she was sure that something was on her husband's mind. She was equally sure that he would tell her the moment he could.

The team under Colonel Abbotson was already at action stations.

By two o'clock in the afternoon the first of the sightseers took up their positions of vantage on the Embankment, on the bridge, every place, in fact, from which they could see the river. The police cleared the streets of any vehicles parked in the main thoroughfare leading to the Embankment. Buses and trains were as crowded coming into London as they normally were, at this hour, going out.

The models went on board at four-thirty.

The jewels went on board at five-thirty.

Hobbs and Gideon approached the Chelsea Pier through the mass of eager Londoners, and Gideon felt a deep disquiet. If a bomb did go off, then the explosion might injure hundreds of spectators, both here and on the pleasure boats, which were already crammed with people. The one reassurance he had was that every conceivable contingency had been anticipated; if there *were* a disaster, the police, ambulances, fire-services, civil defence crews, were there to move in instantly. Police launches were on either side of the river, with reinforcements waiting at every pier. The whole establishment of the special constables of the Thames Division was on duty.

The hawkers called their wares, the children played and blew tin trumpets and let off caps from toy pistols. The newspaper sellers were out in strength.

And the sun shone.

Sir Jeremy Pilkington, and his wife, who looked dazzlingly beautiful, went on board at ten minutes to six, and Gideon and Kate watched them. Penelope and Hobbs were already on board with the other guests, the plain clothes policemen, the Customs men, and the Securial guards.

At five minutes past six, doors beneath the water-line of two barges moored in the roads near Surrey Docks opened; the sound detecting devices of the Royal Marine team picked this up, and immediately started in pursuit of two two-man submarines which were being launched from the barges. Some of Abbotson's team were frogmen, others were in one-man submarines. All of these headed up river. In a few minutes two more, smaller submarines started off from the bowels of a lighter which had been out of service for some months off the Millwall Docks.

On the *River Belle* the parade began.

In the *salon* which was so heavily guarded, the diamonds were handed out to model after model.

The four midget submarines drew closer to the *River Belle* as more of Abbotson's team moved from hiding-places in the Battersea Pleasure Gardens and on the wharves on Chelsea Embankment.

On deck, there was gaiety and applause and wonder.

Down below, Abbotson's men closed in on the raiders, who had no idea that they were suspected until more frogmen came from the *River Casino* and from the banks, giving the raiders no chance at all.

When they were caught, three of them were found to be in possession of limpet mines, each one enough to blow a hole in the *River Belle* and send it to the bottom.

At half-past seven the flotilla began to move down river, and the food and drink, from caviare and champagne to French bread and hot coffee, was served.

"It's *far* better than I expected," Penelope Gideon said, enraptured.

"That's good," agreed Gideon, trying to hide his pre-occupation. As he spoke a plain clothes man came up and gave him a sealed letter. He opened it with great deliberation, his heart in his mouth. It read:

"*You were right. Operation completed. Four arrests made.*" Gideon turned to Hobbs and said gruffly: "That was it, Alec. No need to worry. I'll be back."

He went to the bridge of the old steamer and talked to Singleton and Worby, to Roswell and to Prescott. Every available man was concentrated on the launching sites for the submarines, Screw Smith and Mary Rose were picked up, but the still unidentified stranger remained at large.

He was still at large the next morning.

The frogmen and some of their accomplices ashore were caught in the mammoth raid. The newspapers splashed the story all over their front pages. *The Big River*

Robbery That Never Was became the sensation of the year.

"But we still haven't got the ringleaders," said Gideon to Singleton, two days later. "We can't even be sure that the industrial diamond ring is run by the same people. You've a long haul ahead of you, Chief Inspector."

"I'm used to long hauls, sir."

"Yes. Have you seen Clara Micklewright and her friend Wild lately?"

"Not since the day before last," said Singleton. "You knew Wild was paying for the best legal aid, didn't you?"

"I hoped he was," Gideon said.

In two days' time, Micklewright would come up for a second hearing.

In a few weeks' time, Carter and Cottingham would be on trial at the Old Bailey. Gideon could not see ahead to the time when he would learn that Screw Smith and his gang were employed by a man named Holmann—one of the two men described by St. John—and that they had feared Argyle-Morris had stolen the packet and had discovered their method of smuggling. Once certain he had not, they had simply made sure he could never give evidence against Screw Smith.

He could not know, either, that St. John had been watched so that Screw could be warned in time if he was interrogated by the police; and that when they learned he had been, Holmann and Morro had left the country, directing operations from Holland. These things Gideon would learn later.

But there were things Gideon did know.

Tomorrow, Van Hoorn would be back in London.

Tomorrow, a woman detective officer would start work in the office of Samuel Morris, insurance broker, and would watch Morris's staff.

Tomorrow, Hellier had told him, the Pierces were to go to Australia House and start on the long trail to a new life, with a greater chance of happiness than had seemed possible before.

And tomorrow, so Gideon had promised Kate, he would take a day off, if it were fine, and spend it with her on the banks of the river.

THE END

MYSTERY TITLES IN THE ULVERSCROFT LARGE PRINT SERIES

OCTAVO SIZE

Title	Author
Death of a Ghost	*Margery Allingham*
Death of a Con Man	*Josephine Bell*
The Paton Street Case	*John Bingham*
Death Takes a Detour	*Miles Burton*
Poison in Jest	*John Dickson Carr*
Señor Saint	*Leslie Charteris*
The Saint Around the World	*Leslie Charteris*
Murder in Mesopotamia	*Agatha Christie*
The Clocks	*Agatha Christie*
Ordeal by Innocence	*Agatha Christie*
Cards on the Table	*Agatha Christie*
Lord Edgware Dies	*Agatha Christie*
The Moving Finger	*Agatha Christie*
Death Comes as the End	*Agatha Christie*
Death on the Nile	*Agatha Christie*
Send Superintendent West	*John Creasey*
The Terror Trap	*John Creasey*
Neck in a Noose	*E. X. Ferrars*
Death Knocks Three Times	*Anthony Gilbert*
Death at Traitors' Gate	*Victor Gunn*

The Painted Dog *Victor Gunn*
The Sequins Lost their Lustre
Simon Harvester
Target for Terror *T. C. H. Jacobs*
The Looking Glass War *John Le Carré*
Gideon's Week *J. J. Marric*
Gideon's Risk *J. J. Marric*
Death at the Dolphin *Ngaio Marsh*
The Piper on the Mountain *Ellis Peters*
The Spearhead Death *Maurice Proctor*
Exercise Hoodwink *Maurice Proctor*
The Scarlet Letters *Ellery Queen*
Conflict of Shadows *Colin Robertson*
Murder in the Morning *Colin Robertson*
Time to Kill *Colin Robertson*
The Terrible People *Edgar Wallace*
White Face *Edgar Wallace*
Poison in the Pen *Patricia Wentworth*
Error of the Moon *Sara Woods*
The House at Satan's Elbow
John Dickson Carr
The Borgia Head Mystery *Victor Gunn*
Evil Under the Sun *Agatha Christie*
Moonlight Flitting *Maurice Procter*
The Fourth Side of the Triangle
Ellery Queen
Gideon's Lot *J. J. Marric*
Death of a Doxy *Rex Stout*

Let Him Stay Dead	*T. C. H. Jacobs*
Tycoon's Death-Bed	*George Bellairs*

OTHER MYSTERY TITLES IN THE ORIGINAL ULVERSCROFT LARGE PRINT SERIES

QUARTO SIZE

Black Plumes *Margery Allingham*
A Well Known Face *Josephine Bell*
Death in the Fearful Night *George Bellairs*
Death Paints a Picture *Miles Burton*
The Third Bullet and Other Stories *John Dickson Carr*
Patrick Butler for the Defence *John Dickson Carr*
The Mad Hatter Mystery *John Dickson Carr*
Murder on the Matterhorn *Glyn Carr*
Screaming Fog *John Newton Chance*
The Saint in Europe *Leslie Charteris*
A Lotus for Miss Quon *James Hadley Chase*
Cat Among the Pigeons *Agatha Christie*
4.50 From Paddington *Agatha Christie*
The Mirror Crack'd from Side to Side *Agatha Christie*
Dead Man's Folly *Agatha Christie*
A Caribbean Mystery *Agatha Christie*
Third Girl *Agatha Christie*

At Bertram's Hotel *Agatha Christie*
After the Funeral *Agatha Christie*
The Hound of Death *Agatha Christie*
The Thirteen Problems *Agatha Christie*
Destination Unknown *Agatha Christie*
Murder on the Orient Express *Agatha Christie*
They Came to Baghdad *Agatha Christie*
Murder is Easy *Agatha Christie*
They Do it with Mirrors *Agatha Christie*
Crooked House *Agatha Christie*
Death in the Clouds *Agatha Christie*
Sad Cypress *Agatha Christie*
The Face of the Tiger *Ursula Curtiss*
The Stairway *Ursula Curtiss*
Widow's Webb *Ursula Curtiss*
Selected Adventures of Sherlock Holmes *Sir Arthur Conan Doyle*
The Memoirs of Sherlock Holmes *Sir Arthur Conan Doyle*
The Case Book of Sherlock Holmes *Sir Arthur Conan Doyle*
The Return of Sherlock Holmes *Sir Arthur Conan Doyle*
A Study in Scarlet / The Sign of Four *Sir Arthur Conan Doyle*
Death Comes to Lady's Steps *W. Murdoch Duncan*

Maiden's Prayer *Joan Fleming*
Malice Matrimonial *Joan Fleming*
Prisoner's Friend *Andrew Garve*
The Missing Minx *Richard Goyne*
Exit Harlequin *Cecil Freeman Gregg*
The Crooked Staircase *Victor Gunn*
Death on Bodmin Moor *Victor Gunn*
Black Trinity *T. C. H. Jacobs*
A Deadly Shade of Gold
John D. MacDonald
False Scent *Ngaio Marsh*
Scales of Justice *Ngaio Marsh*
Dead Water *Ngaio Marsh*
Saturday Out *Laurence Meynell*
The Whirl of a Bird *Geoffrey Peters*
Hazard Chase *Jeremy Potter*
The Chief Inspector's Statement
Maurice Procter
Death at the Inn *John Rhode*
Demon's Moon *Colin Robertson*
Peter Gayleigh Flies High *Colin Robertson*
Strong Poison *Dorothy L. Sayers*
Maigret in Society *Georges Simenon*
Maigret and the Young Girl
Georges Simenon
The Jewel of Seven Stars *Bram Stoker*
Danger Under the Moon *Maurice Walsh*
Anna, Where Are You?
Patricia Wentworth

FICTION TITLES IN THE ULVERSCROFT LARGE PRINT SERIES

OCTAVO SIZE

The Promise of His Return *Ruth Aspinall*
In the Absence of Mrs. Petersen *Nigel Balchin*
Whispering Walls *Elizabeth Brennan*
The Portuguese Escape *Ann Bridge*
The Island of Sheep *John Buchan*
Letter from Peking *Pearl S. Buck*
East Wind: West Wind *Pearl S. Buck*
The New Year *Pearl S. Buck*
The Limbo Line *Victor Canning*
The Sands of Mars *Arthur C. Clarke*
The Green Fields of Eden *Francis Clifford*
Love and Mary Ann *Catherine Cookson*
A Song of Sixpence *A. J. Cronin*
Flowers on the Grass *Monica Dickens*
My Friends from Cairnton *Jane Duncan*
The African Queen *C. S. Forester*
Hornblower in the West Indies *C. S. Forester*
Night Without Stars *Winston Graham*
The Four Doctors *John Harley*
The Cross of Lazzaro *John Harris*

The Swan River Story *Phyllis Hastings*
Beauvallet *Georgette Heyer*
The Convenient Marriage *Georgette Heyer*
Mistress of Mellyn *Victoria Holt*
Menfreya *Victoria Holt*
The Wreck of the Mary Deare
Hammond Innes
Campbell's Kingdom *Hammond Innes*
The Lonely Skier *Hammond Innes*
The Doomed Oasis *Hammond Innes*
Ice Cold in Alex *Christopher Landon*
The House in the Dust *Doris Leslie*
Queen in Waiting *Norah Lofts*
Midnight Plus One *Gavin Lyall*
Pray for a Brave Heart *Helen MacInnes*
Fear is the Key *Alistair MacLean*
Where Eagles Dare *Alistair MacLean*
The Dark Crusader *Alistair MacLean*
The Golden Rendezvous *Alistair MacLean*
Maracaibo Mission *F. Van Wyck Mason*
The Flight of the Falcon
Daphne du Maurier
The Blind Spot *Joy Packer*
The Barefoot Mailman *Theodore Pratt*
A Terrace in the Sun *Cecil Roberts*
An Old Captivity *Nevil Shute*
A Savage Place *Frank G. Slaughter*
Shabby Tiger *Howard Spring*

Rachel Rosing	*Howard Spring*
Wildfire at Midnight	*Mary Stewart*
Madam, Will You Talk?	*Mary Stewart*
Thunder on the Right	*Mary Stewart*
Rio D'Oro	*Nigel Tranter*
The Big Story	*Morris West*
Daughter of Silence	*Morris West*
Gallows on the Sand	*Morris West*
Curtain of Fear	*Dennis Wheatley*
Green Hand	*Lillian Beckwith*
Mission in Tunis	*Jacques Pendower*
The Exile	*Pearl S. Buck*
Puppet on a Chain	*Alistair MacLean*
Madselin	*Norah Lofts*
A Ship of the Line	*C. S. Forester*
Bride of Pendorric	*Victoria Holt*
Maddon's Rock	*Hammond Innes*
Dr. Hudson's Secret Journal	*Lloyd C. Douglas*
Monk's Hollow	*John Marsh*
Pied Piper	*Nevil Shute*
The White South	*Hammond Innes*
Faro's Daughter	*Georgette Heyer*
The Deadly Orbit Mission	*F. Van Wyck Mason*
Shooting Script	*Gavin Lyall*
Oh! To be in England	*H. E. Bates*

The Moon-Spinners	*Mary Stewart*
Airs Above the Ground	*Mary Stewart*